The Frog

For Julio   For Claudia

May we all be saved
from the wiles
of the wicked
frog!
And here's to the great
pleasure of new
friendship!
Jack

Prov   May 17, 1996

Books by John Hawkes

JOHN HAWKES

THE

Frog

VIKING

VIKING
Published by the Penguin Group
Penguin Books USA Inc., 375 Hudson Street,
New York, New York 10014, U.S.A.
Penguin Books Ltd, 27 Wrights Lane, London W8 5TZ, England
Penguin Books Australia Ltd, Ringwood, Victoria, Australia
Penguin Books Canada Ltd, 10 Alcorn Avenue,
Toronto, Ontario, Canada M4V 3B2
Penguin Books (N.Z.) Ltd, 182-190 Wairau Road,
Auckland 10, New Zealand

Penguin Books Ltd, Registered Offices:
Harmondsworth, Middlesex, England

First published in 1996 by Viking Penguin,
a division of Penguin Books USA Inc.

1 3 5 7 9 10 8 6 4 2

LIBRARY OF CONGRESS CATALOGING IN PUBLICATION DATA
Hawkes, John, 1925–
The frog : a novel / John Hawkes.
p.   cm.
ISBN 0–670–86577–X (hardcover : alk. paper)
I. Title.
PS3558.A82F76   1996
813'.54—dc20   95–4770

This book is printed on acid-free paper.

Printed in the United States of America
Set in Adobe Garamond
Designed by Francesca Belanger

For Sophie

And from both of us,

with love,

To Pierre and Martine Gault

The Frog

"My dear," said the elegant old lady, a person of truly strung literary temperament, as she paused in her reading and glanced up at the author of the little book in her hands, "I am already beginning to fear for our common morality and even more for the attitude you appear to have assumed toward your country. Is there any nation more culturally fastidious than ours, and hence less deserving of disparagement? So, my dear, I fear the worst. But considering that it is you who have created this . . . inversion"—here her thin smile grew wide —"I shall read to the end. However, I cannot help but add that you are fortunate to be living in this modern day of ours and not in that former time when exile was a fit punishment for less than this! . . ."

CHAPTER ONE

The Tadpole

ON A TRAIN a blind man, armed with dark glasses and white cane, inevitably sits across from the cripple with crutches. The first hears the most fragile sounds of the passing countryside, the other knows he is capable of the swiftest speed. Happily these two converse together, secure within their love of the train. As for me, I am a perfect combination of our afflicted passengers though I have excellent vision and full use of my limbs. It all comes from a good childhood.

I remember distinctly that earliest time of my life, when I was all but newborn—perhaps a year and a half or two years old at most—and the center of everyone's attention on the Domaine Ardente. I accepted without question a situation that was especially agreeable, as if created for me alone, though I was of course unaware of my apparently more than pleasant birthright. My mother, a small trim dark-haired youthful woman more pretty than beautiful, was the first to call me her little Tadpole, though my father immediately joined her in the use of that familiar first name of mine—"How is our little Tadpole today, Marie?" as he used to say—while the inheritor of the Domaine Ardente also seized the privilege from the outset, calling me his little Tadpole quite as if he considered himself my second father. "Good morning, my little Tadpole," he would say upon first seeing me, or "Come along, little Tadpole," he might say in his confident manner, to my mother's evident pride, "let us go study your tiny brethren," and off we would go hand in hand. These two men, the owner of the Domaine Ardente, who presumed to act like my father, and my actual father, were remarkably similar. They were both about forty years old when I was born. They were equally tall, equally broad-shouldered, equally strong of feature, as if those two faces had been cut from the same block of stone. And to cap it all, they were equally gentle in their ways and appeared to partake equally in the most resplendent qualities of manhood.

However, they had their differences. The young count, as he was generally called, was the natural owner of all one thousand hectares of the Domaine Ardente, along with its château and quite elegant farmhouse, where lived our own small modest family of three, and numerous barns and outbuildings. My father, on the other hand, was essentially a farmer. Of course he was an exceptional farmer, a stalwart farmer, a man of sterling character, as he liked to say, and the person in charge of overseeing the farm of the Domaine Ardente, which is saying a lot. The cows, the shaggy work horses, the hordes of squawking chickens, those fields of tomatoes stretching far and wide like a bright red sea—all were his responsibility. Yet I soon came to realize that my father's good nature and devotion to my mother and even more to me amounted to nothing but shyness. He loved us both—wife and Tadpole—yet in the final analysis, which was one of his favorite phrases, and no matter his worthiness, he was from beginning to end a cap-doffer. Yes, he doffed his cap whenever he met the young count, and he was in fact afraid of my mother and me, though in different ways. His strength and subservience to those he loved were a form of timidity, as if the very purity of his love might hurt them, as proved the case. Yes, he was a pure man. A cap-doffer! But in my near infancy I was as proud of my dear little Papa, as I came to call him, as I was of the young count.

Here I should add that dear little Maman, as she soon became to me, had her own well-defined place in the world of the Domaine Ardente, since she was mistress of the young count's kitchen and, small and youthful, trim and pretty and brightly innocent of manner though she was, was nonetheless a cook whose talent was so immense that she might have been an old woman of foulest temper. The young count said that his Marie was like a princess born to the kitchen, a compliment that always made my father smile handsomely and his blue eyes shine. Incidentally, the young count's wife has but a small place in my story—though an explosive place it was—so for now I will only say that she was far more receptive to the world around her than a beautiful young person in her station of life might have been expected to be, and that she was one of those women whose very skin has about it that staggering tightness, as if barely containing the pressure of desire with which it ever so perceptively balloons, very like the golden grape hanging by a thread from the vine. She and the young count were childless.

Ah, but I have neglected a minor but urgent detail. That is, both my father and the young count had heads of extraordinarily black hair, as thick and luxurious as an old mare's black tail. And I might add here that both my father and the young count smoked, cigarettes for the most part but even pipes.

My first breath was of the dense aromatic air born of our peach trees, while my first sense of existence itself was of the boundless nurturing light of the Domaine Ardente. Why, without knowing it, I might very well have been the missing child of the young count and his desirous wife instead of the son of dear little Maman and dear little Papa. But then all four of the principal adults in my earliest life were lucky to have me, and I lucky to have appeared so unexpectedly as the only child, and a tiny squat boy at that, to command, in a sense, the entirety of the Domaine Ardente, no matter my lowly birth. Perfection was mine, harmony was mine, no creature was more highly prized or wielded such power—the invisible power of the first and only offspring. But physically I was the alien of the Domaine Ardente. Small, even for two years old and savoring my second spring, and short and squat and of thick little arms and legs, as, proportionally, I was to remain throughout my days. And to complete my physical self-portrait, I had small, wickedly sharp black eyes that boded no good, as any of them might have seen had they but once shaken themselves loose from the mesmerizing charm I cast about me, so that to a stranger my lively ugliness would have been evident at once. In a glance I would have been exposed as the little frog I was, my very self bearing not the slightest resemblance to the adults most prominent in the Domaine Ardente, or to the unquenchable beauty of the place. But I was not discovered, not betrayed, never recognized as contrary to my circumstances, never as a child of deformity but the opposite, while I bathed and lolled in all the profusion that was mine. At that time no mirror could have revealed the truth. I doted on myself even as I do to this day. Of course I was not actually a frog.

Could any such child of affluence, trotting back and forth between the good things of this earth—all that grew, all that came transformed and fragrant to the table—and the good things subtly evident in the past that flowed in aristocratic veins, possibly have created a hierarchy of the senses? Could I have found one pleasure greater than the next? The sun followed me wherever I went, for me the night held no terror. Quite the contrary. Small birds fell at my feet wherever, in my clumsy fashion, I trod. Was it possible then that I might have formed preferences, been selective in what I loved, found myself more ardent for this or that, more delighted to be in my mother's arms or sitting on my father's lap than running as fast as my chubby legs might carry me straight to the young count as yet hidden behind a corner of the serene château? Yes, I was selective in the midst of bounty, grasping, even, at who or what I loved most. At two years old, or thereabouts, I was severely judgmental about receiving and bestowing pleasure.

Here is the hub of my confession, to be taken any way we wish. At this time of earliest childhood I had two grand passions, the frog pond and my mother. In all my fatty, even grotesque innocence they consumed me, wherever I went, on whomever I smiled. No matter how random my apparent readiness to accept this potent fruit or that one, still my secret yearning—for the frog pond, for my dear little Maman—was the secret that was burgeoning inside me, the ripening secret that was mine alone. No one suspected what the frog pond meant to me or had so much as an inkling—another one of my father's favorite phrases—as to the severity of my love for my girlish mother—not even dear little Maman herself. How I longed to speak out directly to Maman about my love for her. How I regret that I did not. Now it is of course too late. The frog pond has been long obliterated, and my poor young mother has been long gone. As for myself, I am not one to give up his passions easily.

But to lift the edge of one of the layers of the velvet cloth already folded back—I am a complicated simpleton, to say the least!—or to return to a subject already touched on, the dark air I breathed those spring nights when I lay fully awake and smiling to myself, aware of how the shape of my undersized cherrywood bed conformed to the squarish figure it contained, did not merely waft to me the scent of the fruit trees—the air the vehicle, the scent its cargo, as with the bed and myself—but rather was in fact the aroma of the trees themselves. I could not have enjoyed myself more than in my little attic bed in the near-total darkness of those first spring nights, fully conscious of my own plumpness sprawled in rest, the heavy newly washed and ironed sheets—naturally, I was covered only by sheets when in bed that season—and the window open, the night outside filling the space around me with the surprise of darkness and the fleshy smell of the peach trees in the far-off orchards. Of course I would not have bothered to lie awake those nights merely for the sensation of the sheets and the smell of peaches. In fact the air was of more breaths than one. There were apples invisibly opening themselves near the peaches, cherries that apparently could not tell night from day, pears whose night scent was wetter, more moist than that of the peaches, the cherries and apples. And then, finally, the unmistakable aroma of the almond blossoms, which smelled, according to my dear Papa, like fresh manure of such a flowery sweetness that it was fit to adorn any family's dining room table for the ritual of the Sunday midday meal.

Yes, yes, I may well have the growing seasons and times for the flowering of my nocturnal horticultural memories totally confused and at odds with the dictates of farming. Why not? I am no farmer or gardener either.

Nighttime smells, nighttime sights and sounds as well. In my total darkness I used to see the ripe apples glowing as brightly as the glass of red wine that my father lifted on high after extinguishing the smoky lights in our dining room, exclaiming the while about its ruby color that my mother and I could not see, and along with the apples in the orchard of my attic room, as I might say, the peaches and pears also glowed, sometimes coming so close to my face that I might have reached up and touched them. Then I would begin to see the young count's château glowing faintly in the moonlight—of course there was no moon on those nights, how could there have been?—that beautiful bone-colored building with its steeply curved slate roof and its windows that were all open and unlit, except for one in which a figure dressed for the night was always standing. The count? The countess? It made no difference to me. In the next moment I would discover that I was that selfsame figure standing on tiptoe in the window of the sleeping château, and that across from me in the purpling grasses was our own farmhouse, in most respects resembling the château it faced except for its smaller size, its heavy lines, its rougher stone walls and red tile roof, wherein I myself lay musing and dear Maman and Papa lay in the bedroom below me, still murmuring to each other while I, above them, slept soundly—or so they thought. Oh, what a little clairvoyant spy I was!

My father's voice was deep, my mother's high on the register of affection. I knew from everything they did, but especially on those spring nights, that they loved each other nearly as much as they loved me. But never once, as I lay awake in the perfumed darkness of those first nights—I was born in April or perhaps May—did I doubt that my mother ever loved anyone, not even dear little Papa, as much as she did me. And that no one sharing the peaceful life of the Domaine Ardente loved me as much as she did. After all, we were an exemplary mother and son. I followed her about in my miniature stocky way, I had full liberty to join her in the young count's kitchen and to bury my head in her skirts or make it plain—oddly enough I could not talk at the age of two, as I think I was—that I wished a taste of the reddish-brown soup steaming in its porcelain tureen, or one of the little pastries bedded hotly on its silver platter. In the midst of my day's activities I would stop, stand still, then turn and rush off to dear little Maman. Or I would hear her calling me from the kitchen window, for no reason other than to enjoy the sound of my name and the lyrical need for each other that we shared.

My name is Pascal. But for the moment I am still her little Tadpole.

Need I say that my mother read aloud to me in the early evenings before she settled me above in my attic room for the nights I have just described? Of course she did. How not? And what was the subject of the little book she thought most conducive to my nights of sleep? Frogs! Yes, frogs! In my life I have always been caught like an insect in this or that web of coincidence left spanning a dark corner of one after another abandoned building. But what pleasure to be left hanging as the sticky captive in the center of the silvery web! And to me there is no difference between a spider's web and a frog pond.

Here I see that we have arrived at precisely the moment to ask the crucial question as to which of the fair twins, of night, of day, was brighter—back, that is, when the door was first set ajar for my exit from the amniotic waters. Up shoot the hands! The answer—it is such an obvious question—is shouted forth on piping wings of derision. The fool, they imply, how can we tolerate such condescension? Well, let them go follow the way of the world, which is smugness and certainty, their little bottoms happily stuck to their benches. Because if I choose to do so, I may well say that brightness does not depend on degrees of light, that the day is in fact as dark as night and the night as wonderfully lit up as day. Reason? Coherence? Oh, but let me defend myself, will you? I would like to pass by coherence and say at once that reason is the true demon, the devil that breathes most hotly down my back or my neck, whichever expression is the least grating, the most tolerable—clearly it makes no difference to me—as I go my way, which is not—not, I repeat— the way of the world. So much for obviousness. At least I have the right to define myself as the most nonconforming of all the conformists who crowd into our urine-smelling rooms of learning. What is the school if not our world? And the difference between day and night is simply a matter of active versus passive good humor. Not at all a matter of what can be seen and heard and done but, in all these things, a question of quality. In sleeping I sighed eagerly to myself, I met the daylight with little cries of delight that were inseparable from the alertness that released my babyish heroic limbs to action. The small cries with which I awoke, as the new sunlight turned my white sheets to orange and warmed the thick wooden beams above my bed, made me a fair likeness, in the prime of my time after infancy, to the brazen self-centered cock whose crowing always preceded my first shrill tinkling cries. The open window was my first station, where, for an instant, I would rest my elbows on the sill and survey the entire sunlit kingdom of the Domaine Ardente: the fields stretching far and wide beneath their blinding coverings of dew, the long rows of firewood mathematically stacked and promising a still different order of plenitude. And of course the young count's château, which, standing full in its allotment of sunlight that was far greater than that in which our farmhouse was rooted—an inequality I happily accepted—was no longer bone-colored as it had been only minutes before, but was a small stately composition of fair stone turned the color of mustard, or dried tobacco leaves, or the soft gold of the count's ring, or a combination of all three as blended from nature's wet palette. Finally, there was a two-wheeled cart awaiting its shaggy horse, and faint streamers of smoke rising from the château's three chimneys, lifting themselves aloft symmetrically for the sake of the smoke sure to come, sure to disappear.

These were the first signs of the day's good humor

that set my little elbows to dancing on the sill where they rested. Then a sudden rush to the porcelain pot, large as an adult's, pure white, thick, heavy, tastefully girdled with bright flowers, rimmed with a comfortable round lip and sporting a fine handle, that faithfully awaited my most pressing needs day and night, but especially at the break of day, behind the door of my very own bedside commode. In those days I may not have been able to talk, but at least I was as well versed as an adult in the fundamentals required of both the child and the adult he would become. A clean and thoughtful creature, beyond a doubt. And one endowed with fierce energy.

"Why, Marie, our little Tadpole cannot keep still for a moment!"—which was not exactly true since I could sit as still as a stone on my father's warm lap, as long as I found him entertaining, and furthermore, whenever I was in the proximity of dear little Maman, especially when she was reading aloud to me one of my favorite stories—yes, about a frog!—I became as round and fat and flaccid as a pillow. Yet on the surface my father's buoyant exclamations about my constant activity, even in merely lifting a spoon to my wide mouth, as madly impatient as a new and featherless bird, shaking my spoon all over the place, were true. On the surface he was justified in the vital good humor, the parental surprise, with which he called attention to what they had all noticed from the moment I had first appeared—namely, that my every movement, from twitching to running, was more pronounced, to put it mildly, than the irrepressible energy of any of the myriad scrawny children you may wish to choose for comparison.

So yes, I twitched. And yes, I did run about uncontrollably. But Papa was wrong. He should not have been amused. He should not have constantly voiced aloud his long-familiar observation in those tones of his that conveyed as much anguish as happy pride, as my dear little Maman already knew. No indeed. In the presence of my inability to keep still he should have felt only terror. And should have spoken of my inability to be at rest not in shrugging tones of jubilation but in the soft voice of terror itself. After all, the violence latent in my boisterousness—"There he goes, Marie! Off like a shot!" —was the first sign. Dear little Papa, always the handsome, anxious jokester. Blind as a bat!

Which of course reminds me of the blind man and cripple riding happily together across our green countryside on that rickety train. Father and son, no doubt. As long as we're here, we might as well stick to this unpleasant subject a moment longer. If I had my way, there would be no fathers in this world of ours, but only sons. It's a nice thought no matter how vehemently it is denied me. Then too, and despite my complaining—complain! complain! I am famous for nothing if not picking away at the edifice!—my Papa did very well for himself as fathers go. His great size was not a threat but a comfort. His rubber boots, taller by far than I myself was at that time, and inevitably covered by great gouts of mud, proclaimed for all to see that he was, yes, a farmer, and yet also testified to his fastidious nature, for they always stood just inside

our front door, though my mother would have preferred
that he leave them without. A farmer, a manager, an over-
seer. A strong kindly man who, had he possessed the
young count's enviable history, might also have been a
man of fine breeding—there indeed was one of the best-
loved phrases in his stable!—and a man of learning as well.
A little anxious, no doubt of it. And shy? Even a bit stiff,
or I might go so far as to say prudish, in the face of privacy
or the heady seductive rose of intimacy. Let him just come
upon me when I was unavoidably confined to my overly
large pot, which, despite its size, was nonetheless a perfect
match for my plump bottom, which never sat on a school
bench, I can assure you, and you've never seen such a
display of shy awkwardness, as if he had stumbled upon
the young countess herself in the nude—and what a
frightful scene that would have been!—with his cap in his
hand and our young lady surprised though oddly receptive
in her warm pool. Yet contradictorily, there were times of
fading or rising light when I might appear at exactly some
inconvenient moment when my mother, dressing, un-
dressing, would pause, silk in hand, and as sweetly as possible urge me back to my attic room or outside to scatter
the ducks. Whereupon my poor Papa would argue the
opposite, bestowing upon us both his ill-advised magna-
nimity. "Oh, let him stay, Marie. He's only a tadpole!"
At which dear Maman would shake her head quizzically
—never, never opposing him—and continue with her
business until the leg I had been staring at disappeared or

more of my Maman than I care to say for the moment
came to view.

Modesty? Modesty? Oh come, you must leave even
me a little elbow room in which to breathe. Just wait until
I suddenly puff myself up and reveal all! I can turn a face
redder than one of the tomatoes reddening in deserved
embarrassment in the fair hand of the young countess.
You'll see.

Now, if my father was an honest rarity in his own
small family, a tall man, a black-haired man, who could
not have been more appreciative of Maman and me,
though also fearful, as I have said—repetition being my
hallmark, as you've surely learned by now—of the more
intimate needs of Maman and me, and being something
of a pretender to manhood as well as to being the kind
of burly man who likes to leave mud on his rubber
boots—his good humor, I must insist, ran the gamut from
honest blue-eyed optimism to that kind of humor that
comes within a hair of falling over the brink into the very
pit of vulgarity that he abhorred. For instance, if anyone,
from sophisticated plowman to crude butcher, mentioned
a cold fish in his bed, my father would blush as brightly
as the young countess's tomato. But he too liked to joke,
my Papa, as large and pleasantly reserved as he was. Sometimes, at the start of day, he would draw me to his side
and lean so closely to me that I could smell his breath,
which was as sweet as that of one of his white cows, and
enclose me in his immensity and stoop so as to put his

mouth to my ear. "Pascal," he would say, with my given name treating me like a true adult and one worthy of receiving the confidence at hand, "your grandmaman, my fortunate Pascal, has twenty—mind you!—two— mind you—teeth!" By the use of pauses he would inject into this absurdity a nearly recognizable kinship to that genuine joke at which we nearly explode into a spluttering of unwilling laughter or tremble and stand back helplessly. At these times my father always smiled, though more to himself than at me. Then he would push me gently back into the living world, and off we would go on our separate ways. I would hear him repeating to himself that silliness, always on the verge of laughter, until he disappeared. In my stuffy childish pragmatism, I hated those words, which were so very far afield of the seriousness that was mine and that I cherished.

Your grandmaman has twenty-two teeth! Twenty-two teeth has your grandmaman!

The joke was that I had no grandmother at that time, since both my father's mother and my mother's mother died almost simultaneously and only months before my first appearance in the famous frog pond or forbidden garden, as you will. I much regretted their absence. Had they been living, all three of us would have benefited from their bright wholesomeness and Sunday dinners. No doubt their sweetness and the fact that both these nice old ladies were destined to die with a full complement of real teeth in their heads would have stopped my father from indulging in his silly irreverence, which, at the time, I resented, as I have said, though I was more than flattered to be included within the embrace of Papa's well-intended confidence. Beyond his joke he was not able to express his fatherly love of me, though he tried hard enough, and back then when I had barely risen from my life in the pond, so to speak, I was delighted to have his slightest attention. At any rate Papa's good humor throve in daylight. He loved the openness of field and well-hunted wood, the manliness of the broad sun. He had no use, as he used to say, for anything underhanded, by which he meant all that he could not see, anticipate, readily comprehend with a bland smile. He did not like shadows. The very idea of secrecy made him frown. He was the archenemy of deceit, a word he much loved for the sake of the anger it aroused in him. He would have made a good judge, had he not been born to the farm, poor Papa. In a word, my father was not a man of the night, which included darkness itself and whatever might smack of femininity. He was forever trying to persuade the young count to order the draining of my beloved frog pond. Imagine being offended by stagnant water! And this from the very man devoted to the yearly job of removing the shit—it was a vulgarism that did not come readily to him but which he therefore used with greater frequency than was necessary and with feigned gusto—removing the shit, then, that had collected both at the château and at our farmhouse as well. He had a true liking for excrement and, laughingly, would give us a lengthy discourse at the drop of a hat—yes, again, again!—on the differences between cow dung and horse manure. But let him not step outside in the darkness!

In point of fact there was not a single frog pond on the Domaine Ardente, there were many, all connected by little throatlike passages or trickling streams. And darkness? Secrecy? All I could want. Oak trees grew at the edges of these ponds, their roots bulging out like goiters from the dank earth where it dropped off into the sluggish water; and wherever they could find footing between the oaks—oh yes, they may well have been live oaks, may well have been—and selfish bramble bushes, broad weeping willows helped to enclose my frog pond, which I prefer to speak of in the singular, since there was one pond more appealing to me than all the others put together and where I most liked to squat and crouch in my own childish time out of time. How shrouded it was, my frog pond! How dark and cool—yet sultry too—even in one of the sudden warm hours that settled down that spring on the Domaine Ardente. Once I had made my way to my frog pond, I became as still as the frog I awaited, as unmoving as the water lilies that spread across the scummy or muddy surface of the pond. It was cool, it was warm, it was a place of midnight in the fullest part of the day. Here and there the oaks, the willows, the screens of bushes, admitted tiny shafts of light that suddenly engaged in brief skirmishes, reflecting, crisscrossing, attacking each other before being just as suddenly extinguished in this daily night that was not determined by church bell or any sort of heavenly system. At least not when I hid in the depths of my frog pond at the height of the daylight hours. Of course the rank darkness was different at sunrise or dusk. For most of the day, however, I could count on finding this special, even illicit dimness, perhaps a smelly total absence of light in which it was hard even to make out the fleshy lily pads, whenever I had the whim or determination to go fiercely into the bright nocturnal world of my frog pond. So I crouched, or squatted, or stretched myself out flat on my belly, eyes at a level with the edge of the pond, immobile, silent, intent, undetectable to anyone passing by or to the creatures of the frog pond itself. I watched, I listened. The dragonflies hovered and dashed about the thick surface with a deafening roar of their little engines, the lily pads tempted me to reach out and touch their oily skins. Inevitably there was one in particular that I concentrated on, an immense beast as flat as a plate and apparently glued to the surface, so tight it was to the water that, like so many of its brethren, it decorated. This grande dame of lily pads was large and of a blackish, greenish, dark bluish color, a thick creature composed of a soft pulp dressed in a gleaming skin as inviting as the water that kept it lubricated. She was a mystery, my awesome lily pad, and ancient, as was evident by the broad indifferent wrinkles or undulations that so beautifully contradicted her apparent flatness. Touch it? Oh, I was tempted to get into that productive water somehow, by slipping or falling, and entrust myself to the pack of them, violating them all with my fresh stubby fingers until at last I reached my fair queen, great flowering receptive mass, and touched it, pinched it, perhaps caressed it like the small startled boy I might have been in the bedchamber of the young count's wife.

Far-fetched? The height of improbability? Well, you will soon see just how close I came to being so ensnared. It was an alluring fright, I can tell you.

But all this was the crudest of my spring fantasies, for I respected beyond my own life my favorite lily pad, which floated indolently just out of reach. It was only the imagined sensation of touching her that enthralled me, since it was the lily pad's sensuous invulnerability that kept me still, that held my gaze. Yes, I was almost angry with passion, such a marvelous living thing was this ancient lily pad in her ballroom of fecundity and slime. There were the various trees and growths attempting to drown themselves in slow motion in these fetid waters, there was the occasional inexplicable patch of clear water and rent in the trees and brambles that caused a clear mirrorlike reflection of blue sky replete with a few clouds and little bird to lie before me and to divert my attention from the reality of darkness and worms and water flowerings that seemed to invite my mouth as well as my eyes. There was a curious truncated tree that proved, on closer inspection, to be two stumps grown so thickly together that I thought of their rotten sculpture as two old ladies hugging each other.

And in the center of it all the empty platter of the empty queen. I watched that lily pad for the sheer illicit pleasure of watching—is there so great a difference between a lily pad and Diana? Let it go, then. For of course

I had an ulterior motive in fixing my eyes for half an afternoon on that unctuous thing undulating in the water. In my scowling fashion I loved its emptiness, but I loved that old noble demimondaine more when all at once plop! And there would be a frog, a big frog, squatting in its very center. If at that moment my ancient stately lily pad had been able to draw her bed curtains, she surely would have. As for myself, in that dripping instant I knew what it was to act the spy!

All the while that I was so engaged in concentrated, furtive study of my lily pad I was of course awaiting the black frog. What could you expect? After all, I was only a two-year-old boy, whose passions, with which unknowingly he was all but bursting, could hardly have reached the degree of consciousness and sophistication that I have not restrained myself from articulating. No indeed. I was just a small boy waiting to spy on a frog. But far from innocent. I was robbed of innocence at birth, though I suspect that back then, at the dawn of skepticism, many children were born missing their innocence. As for now, well, you'd be lucky to find an innocent babe in a thousand. If you wanted one, that is.

The point is that I was never able to catch the frog in the act of emerging from the muddy depths and plopping himself down on his favorite lily pad and mine. I stared for hours, I clenched my fists, I scowled, my angry willpower puffed out my round cheeks that dear little Maman so loved to stroke. I readied myself to see the invisible frog's exact entrance into view, to see him shoot up suddenly with a flying leap and land safely on the lily pad, or to see first his head, then shoulders, then hoary arms, and to be witness to his ignoble struggle to haul himself up and out of the clinging water to safety on the spongy plate waiting to serve him up to my scrutiny. But I could not. As long as I watched, like a child determined to keep his eyes open so as not to fall asleep, I was unable to maintain a perfect vigil. Never did I entrap my majestic frog in my spying. Never. Nor could I detect my instant of failure, the chink in my armor. I was capable of holding watch for most of a day without the slightest trembling or consciousness of my remarkable feat. And I did not blink. In fact I was born incapable of blinking, which a few people, but only a few, noted with appropriate discomfort. At any rate I did not lose sight of the empty lily pad in the slowly changing light, was diverted by nothing, no matter the overly curious bird that might make its way into the seclusion of the frog pond, never again to fly free, no matter that another portion of the embankment might slide loose and disappear beneath the brownish surface, thereby leaving naked still another entanglement of virgin roots. By these slow contractions of the frog pond I was not diverted. Such patience was nothing less than satanic, especially in light of my general inability to maintain stillness. Yet so it was and so I failed. One moment my superb attention would be fixed on the maddening vacancy of the lily pad, the next I would be staring at the frog, who— yes!—was there, so heavily filling that vacancy that the lily pad seemed threatened with sinking. But he was there, as large as my head and as slimy as if he had been sitting on that lily pad and fruitlessly attempting to dry himself in the sun all afternoon.

There must have been signs. The dragonflies must have shut down their engines and in an instant settled to the surface as if never again to rise. The trapped bird must have made some sort of strangled sound in its tiny throat. Surely there was some such sign of warning, no matter how sudden, how brief, how apparently insignificant, that the awesome frog was about to make himself visibly known in the frog pond once again. If so, such a flurry of heralding minutiae escaped me.

For as long as I studied him on this or that afternoon, my mouth going dry and my small black eyes starting from my head, my bold frog steadfastly refused to return my gaze, until just before his disappearance, that is, though not always, which is to say that he was not predictable, sitting as if a veritable cannonade would not shake him loose, yet all the while as aware of me as I was of him.

A big wet creature seemingly composed of slime that oozed the day long through what must have been tiny pores in his leathery skin, he was in appearance that shiny and repellent, which made him all the more attractive to me. He held himself half sitting up with great effort. Midway between sun and stagnant water he blazed in his glorious colors of putrefaction—dark green, dark blue, black. He moved so little that even his efforts to breathe frightened me. I thought that inside the flat sack of him he had no bones. He looked like a bat. But oh, he might have been wearing a crown, that frog! How I loved him.

It was not merely to see him that I spent so many days at the frog pond. It was to see his eyes. By and large he kept them averted. He allowed me, so to speak, full view of his webbed feet, the sharp ridges that revealed the hairlike bones inside him, or even moved his great head a degree or so to the left, to the right, interested, that moment, in something other than me. But to that masterful frog his eyes were sacred, as I well knew. For hours he sat there as if deliberately waiting me out. On some days, after engaging me in hours of the most painful study—and to think that I was never an apt pupil, let alone a scholar!— he would deny me altogether and disappear from view by whatever sleight of hand was his, before allowing me one glimpse of his eyes. But on other days, toward the end of our hours together or at once, while he was still dripping profusely on his lily pad, fresh in arrival, he would suddenly turn his head or even inch his fat body around until—yes!—there they were, his eyes, meeting mine. It was then, even as I could feel my wide mouth smiling still wider in my elation, that all at once I was overcome with utter abasement and wanted only to wriggle, to move, to flee, to escape the dominion of the frog's eyes. But could not. And not once did that frog blink at me!

Have you ever been stared at by a frog?

When a frog looks deep into a child's eyes, he does so with such impassive recognition in that gaze of his that the child cannot help but be overcome by guilt, by terror, yet by amazement as well. I should know. One glance into my frog's large black unlidded eyes, as they first appeared, and I had not the slightest doubt but that some terrible doom had befallen me, and that that secret doom was mine to carry within my person forever. A lifelong treasure that I could just as well have done without—or so I thought at my worst moments, which did not last long.

My frog's name was Armand.

And here we are! Back to the endless springtime of my nights in bed, back to the stories—about a frog named Armand, of course—that my mother used to read to me as preparation for sleep. I did not lie in the sumptuous hollow of my fresh sheets merely smelling and watching the darkness in which Maman and Papa thought I lay above them safely asleep. Not at all. One of my profoundest nighttime pleasures was listening to the night as well. To what? Oh yes, to the distant frogs. In the night it surrounded me, engulfed me, far off, close to my open window, that sound of contented croaking that only the frogs could make. It was a chorus now soft, now loud, now timid, now bold, chaotic yet formed into the shape of a song, a lullaby without beginning or end, a natural hypnosis more soothing than that of any other nighttime sounds I heard—whether of owls, cicadas, or falling rain. And as long as it lasted, which was as long as I stayed awake, in its midst I always detected the authoritative croaking of Armand. He made no sound when we were together. In the daytime I saw in his eyes the sounds he made at night in his throat, or rather in the smell of those spring nights I strained to hear the sounds of Armand giving voice to what I had seen in his eyes in the daylight. There is a difference. At night the imperious Armand was but one frog in ten thousand, and at their center I gave myself up to them, vulnerable to their swarming upon me yet safe from them all, the sole listener enjoying their song.

It all began just after dusk, when Maman would tell me that it was time to have our nightly frog story, and up we would go, dear little Papa dismissing us with a flourish of his most generous fatherhood.

There was my nightshirt, cut from the same material as my thick sheets permeated with the overpowering smell of cleanliness, and an oil lamp, and a small wooden chair, and the open window. At this point I would be more eager than dreamy, while Maman would be smiling and shaking her head of dark curls in anticipation of what we were about to share. "Remember, Pascal," she would say, "only one story! You mustn't ask Maman for another." Readily I would agree, smiling my smile that was so much wider than hers, settling myself into my square bed, though I was never exactly at peace with myself, looking at dear little Maman and hoping that the expression on my face was pleasing her. Slowly she would open the book and begin the story. Beneath her voice—I hear it still—the sound of the frogs would be nothing more than the softest stirring of the night outside.

"The Stories of Armand the Frog" concerned a little girl named Vivonne, her bad-tempered friend, Henri, and Armand himself, who, as Vivonne well knew, was that lovely child's brother transformed into an ugly frog, as if all frogs were not ugly, despite that sentimental majority who persist in viewing the frog as small or even precious, that detestable word. But how typical of most children's stories, yet not quite, thanks to that peculiar tuck in its side, like my bat turned frog. Why, those stories might have been closer to life, as they say, had that magical frog proved to be not Vivonne's brother but her father. However, there we are, and my nightly immersion in "The Stories of Armand the Frog" was so complete that I myself might have been both frog and brother. Naturally Vivonne, with her imperturbably good disposition and dark curly hair much like my mother's, could talk to the frog and knew that one day she herself would transform her beloved Armand, which was how she felt about him, back into her dear brother. Her only task was to overcome her repugnance for the frog, and—pouf!—there, in a puddle, would stand her brother in all his glory, dripping from the years he had spent disguised in the frog pond. However, and in delicious fulfillment of every child's expectation, Vivonne felt such abhorrence for Armand the frog that she despaired of ever doing what she was destined to do in her pretty life, whether she wanted to or not, though she had in fact learned to let Armand sit in the palm of her cupped hand, trembling the while and biting her lip, despite her love for the ugly creature that looked up at her with imploring eyes. In rapture I listened to the tale of Armand, Vivonne, Henri, and the gypsy woman, or of the frog, the children, and the one-armed traveler, and there was one, I remember, about the frog, the children, and another frog. What a delight it was, how instructive! My small bright eyes were as tightly fixed on my mother's lively face as they had been fixed on Armand the real frog only that afternoon or the one before. My mother read aloud those stories with all the sounds of artistry that a pretty woman could bring to bear on a story whose simple tones and vivid events could bring so much pleasure exactly suited to a child fully awake yet on the verge of sleep. Her curls trembled, her soft voice was as clear as the water at the bottom of our well, she was an actress for whom the story that issued from her pretty mouth was peopled with an endless variety of small creatures, all holding tiny hands or fleeing each other. She would turn a page, Armand would beg Vivonne to allow him once again to sit in her cupped palms, Henri would come rushing to interrupt their reluctant tryst with a stick. Remember the tale of Armand the frog and Bocage the crow? What happiness!

One day the crow, who was of course ten times the size of the frog, challenged Armand to a singing contest. Henri, forever on the ready to thwart the frog however he could, demanded to be the judge, since, there being little to choose between the cawing of a crow and the croaking of a frog, Henri's own word would clearly determine the outcome in the crow's favor, thereby casting ignominy on the frog and in turn spiting once more the little girl Vivonne in all her partiality to Armand. The chosen day arrived, the contestants assembled just out of earshot of a little brook and near a wild flowering of blueberry bushes. Henri scowled and folded his arms judiciously, Vivonne said that she could not bear to see Armand suffer so severe a defeat and would absent herself from the field, though in fact she cleverly hid behind the blueberry bushes. Bocage declared himself the first to sing and preened his great black feathers, strutted in a circle on his two shiny yellow legs, and then, in a long and prideful display of grandeur, as he thought, began to caw as long and loudly as he could. His feathers shook, four nearby cows kicked up their heels and fled, the wicked little boy Henri nearly covered his ears with his hands but managed not to. Surely no uglier sound could have filled the day, pleasing the crow no end but making the poor frog cower. At last the self-satisfied crow ceased his terrible performance and took his bow. Then it was the frog's turn, which Henri anticipated with smug self-satisfaction, though he continued to scowl as if in the total objectivity required of any judge in a contest. Bocage the crow stood back, Armand the frog hopped upon a small rock, thereby hoping to gain whatever advantage he could, which was little. There was silence, there was sunlight, the distant cows turned to listen, the boastful crow smiled to himself and waited. At last Armand filled his little body to bursting and opened wide his mouth and began to sing. But what song was this? What sweetness coming forth from the mouth of a frog? Oh, not at all the monotonous painful croaking that the boy, the crow, and the attentive cows had expected to hear. Oh, just the opposite! For the frog on the rock was in fact singing in the cheerful melodic voice of a little girl! The cows drew near, the defeated crow flapped about in angry circles, his feathers flying, while after a moment the wicked little boy, his eyes meaner than ever and his face red, leapt at the frog, chasing the little creature off his rock and into the tall grass, and then—for of course Henri had understood the trick at once—ran to the blueberry bushes and caught the laughing Vivonne by her curly hair. The now frightened crow flew up to a branch of a nearby tree, again the cows fled, Vivonne struggled unsuccessfully to escape the angry embrace of the wicked boy. But before the boy could harm the little girl, or do anything more than to disturb her clothing, Armand hopped back onto the sunny rock and, as the defeated crow flew off after the cows, caused the bad-tempered Henri to free Vivonne and yawn, grow weary, and, overcome by the powers of sleep, lie down beside the brook. . . .

And the rest? The second half of the story? Oh, there was Armand hiding himself in Henri's pocket while the boy slept, there was the waking of the wicked boy, the discovery of the frog in his pocket, a great commotion, Henri's escape from both the frog and his terror, thanks to Vivonne, who commanded him to drop his trousers and run—silly boy—and finally the sound of Vivonne's laughter at the resultant plight of the now stumbling Henri, at whom she stared with suddenly sober attention, while the victorious frog hopped back into the brook to await his next encounter.

Most of the nightly tales that I remember from "The

Stories of Armand the Frog" contained adventures similar
to this one. Inevitably Henri lost his trousers, inevitably
Henri the wicked boy would hop about in rage, the little
frog clinging for dear life to one of the boy's bare buttocks
while Vivonne smiled or frowned and filled her eyes with
the sight of Henri's whirling frightened nakedness. Did it
ever end, that collection of stories in the ancient book that
sat so prettily in the hands of dear little Maman throughout those spring nights of my childhood? That volume
from which there issued the sound of my mother's voice
precisely as Vivonne's childish soprano voice arose from
the mouth of the frog or as the song of the choirboy comes
from the score he holds and not his mouth? Surely there
must have come the final night, the last story in the book,
when the song of the distant frogs grew faint with sadness
and faded to nothing, and the last few words drifted off
onto the vastness of the spring air and my mother ceased
reading, smiled down at me, and shut the book. Forever.
Oh yes, that book I loved, fragrant with my mother's
touch and redolent with the life of the frog who was the
namesake of the real frog who so consumed my own life,
must have had a conclusion.

No doubt Vivonne finally allowed Armand into her
bed one night and twitched and squirmed, shivered and
trembled, slept and woke as in a dream, shockingly aware
of the little wet creature touching her here and there or,
worst of all or best, suddenly hiding in the bedclothes,
lost, unaccountable, waiting to resume his tickling of Vivonne's pure young body until she dozed, drifted partially

awake, crying out in her little girl's ravaged voice as there
in the new sunlight she lay, no longer a child, of course,
but a young woman, despite her still youthful appearance.
And the frog? He stood at the foot of her bed, of course,
no longer a frog but the promised brother, who should
have been a prince according to the dictates of most stories
about frogs and children, but was not. Here "The Stories
of Armand the Frog" must disappoint us, for that stalwart brother, when finally he shed his ugliness, or rather
when our dear Vivonne recognized that same ugliness for
the shining beauty that it was—male beauty, that is—
emerged not as a prince, as he rightfully deserved, but in
the form of an ugly old king smiling down upon his prize.
But did the radiant Vivonne, sprawled out on her damp-
ened bed without a thought to modesty, share our own
shock and disappointment at this final gift of her story?
She did not. After all, an ugly old king was better than
nothing, if she could not have her prince, as apparently
she could not, and she had already learned that the mighty
powers of a frog will never suffer the rules of convention.

Oh, let me be honest, though honesty is nearly as
repugnant as rationality. However, I do not remember that
"The Stories of Armand the Frog" ever reached a conclusion or that dear Maman ever ceased her nightly reading.
The curious fact of the matter, and this I do remember
with undeniable certainty, is that for the longest while I
was satisfied to allow my mother to read to me one story
a night instead of demanding that she spend the entirety
of each of those spring nights with her son and her book,

as I might have done, though soon enough I contrived to manage even that. But patience is a virtue I require of others if not myself.

Well, there we have it. Benevolent father, adoring mother, young count and countess who considered us indispensable to the Domaine Ardente, which I was intended to dominate, and finally the frog Armand, who belonged to me alone, for better or worse—all the ingredients, as I promised, of the good childhood which at the outset I declared had been mine. But wait! Is there not more? Some essential factor missing? Ah, let me not neglect Christophe, my only friend but my friend nonetheless. No account of a good childhood can be complete without a childhood friend, and far be it from me to overlook that little boy who might as well have been my twin—though opposite to me in every way—so strong were the bonds between us in those first idyllic days of mine.

Yes, I, Pascal, was granted a friend by the unaccountable good fortune into which I was born, and what a friend! Poor little Christophe. It was as if his wretched conception and birth had occurred merely that he might be my companion, when I wished the companionship of someone other than adults or frog, and also that he might take unto himself all the evils that would have come down ferociously upon my own head had he not existed. His was the weakness to my strength, the misery to my self-satisfaction, the defeat and sadness to my invulnerability, the cry of pain to my regal pout.

He was as small as an insect, as weak as a spider, a tiny ageless boy who sniveled incessantly and wore large round opaque spectacles. And fear? Why, he was afraid of his own shadow, as the saying goes, and with reason, for Christophe's shadow was a ghastly thing to see, with legs and arms half the thickness of Christophe's actual limbs, which were thin enough, and spindly, black, the poor arms often held outstretched from that wisp of a shadow-body never at rest, and from the ends of which there dangled elongated hands ending not in tiny fingers but in claws, or so it seemed as those brittle uncontrollable hands flapped about to the unheard music of his persecution. That evil mother of his was quite right when she accused Christophe of being afraid of his own shadow, though it was Christophe's own mother, again the exact opposite of mine, who inflicted upon him the humiliation that was all he knew. She was fairly young, like my mother, and wore her black hair tight to her head. And oh, the things she said to my little friend! It never failed but that when I paid Christophe a visit, I would find that woman turning him out-of-doors with imprecations that made even my own stalwart approach to their wreck of a farmhouse falter. How he would cower, poor Christophe, while his half-dressed mother lounged in the doorway and assured him that he was not her own son and that soon he would strangle and die slowly and lie dead at her feet, thanks, as she said, to the hatred she bore him. As for Christophe's father, he was as much the victim of his wife as was the son of the mother.

"That woman is at it again," my father would occasionally say at our midday meal. "Jacques is not in the fields today, simply because that woman is once again whipping his buttocks, as the men say, with the very belt intended to hold up the trousers fallen about his ankles. It's a disgrace."

"But Michel-André," my Maman would reply in her saddest, most serious voice, "perhaps you shouldn't speak of it in Pascal's presence."

"Tadpole knows more about that family than I do, Chérie. It is to our own son's credit that he chooses to befriend that poor little lad, though the young count calls that family the only blight on the Domaine Ardente and will one day get rid of them—man, woman, and child. Mark my words. You know it is rumored that even the best of my men take time from their work in order to inquire after the man of the place—if man he is—and then stay to enjoy the woman. I tell you, Marie, it is a disgrace."

Was it because of what my father said that I made my visits to Christophe as short and infrequent as they were? Was I afraid of the cries of Christophe's own father, which so often rang from within the near-ruined house along with the sounds of leather belt on fiercely welted flesh, as I imagined it to be? Or was it because the face of Christophe's mother sometimes appeared at the edge of a slightly drawn curtain when the half-blackened farmhouse came into view, and I felt her eyes upon me—calm, appraising, as crafty as the rare partial smile on her white face? She was not an ugly-looking woman, not at all, but capable at any moment of a rage that was all her latent beauty could resort to, even as it promised, oddly enough, the oval face of the young count's wife. No, it was simply that I wished to preserve my privacy at any cost and intended beyond a doubt to prevent my strange little friend from intruding into my own life. Not for Christophe the slightest glimpse of my frog pond. Never! I paid my visits to him only for my own benefit, liking him as much as I would have liked any other small boy, and in a way enjoying the drama of his plight. What a curious-looking little pair we must have made as side by side, the one shriveled to the ultimate wisp of a child, the other as well-fed, well-loved, and hefty as he could have been, we marched bravely, so to speak, up and down the rutted road, careful to avoid the dog on his chain and no doubt pretending to confer about some military tactic or other in a silence broken only by my own proud muteness and Christophe's whimpering. Once the poor little creature tried to clutch my hand, and for that I denied him so much as a sight of me until once again, and when I had all but forgotten my ill-fated friend, my father spoke of him one day at the table, and I remembered Christophe and relented. Perhaps if I had known that my rapidly approaching affliction would prove far greater than Christophe's torments, I might have befriended him in a less selfish fashion. Nonetheless we had our adventures together, and rarely did I return from seeing him without feeling still better than ever about the self that lived inside my buttery skin. There's nothing like misery to enhance tenfold someone else's already triumphant state of well-being.

Affliction? Well, there it is at last, the magic cat that jumps from my bag of tricks, the doom its victim suffers and by which he thrives. I have mentioned that there was more than one sign of its latency, and so there was. For instance, there was the day when in a gesture so swift and unexpected that even I could not see it, let alone Papa, with my wide-flung arm, though perhaps it was my chubby hand for all I know, I swept Papa's glass of red wine from the table as if some unnatural force had snatched up that glass of wine and sent it flying. One moment Papa's *ballon* of wine, a most inviting light red color for all the sunlight it had absorbed, rested within easy reach of his fingertips, or in fact tempting his large hand so that it had already risen and was on its way toward the glass of wine, a kind which incidentally my dear little father particularly enjoyed, then, suddenly exempt from all laws of time and physics, that glass leapt from its place beside Papa's plate of ham and country bread and flew across the room to shatter on the far wall.

"Why, Michel-André," said dear little Maman with a laugh, "you have knocked over your glass!"

He was a lovely sight, my giant of a father, his jovial spirit brought low in utter clumsiness by what he could not understand and the sight of the wine, no longer appealing to his expectations as it had been but a moment before, trickling down the stone wall like blood from a finger.

"But Marie," he said at last, "I did not touch my glass!" And then, understanding flooding his face like the sunlight in which it bathed, "Why, I believe that little Pascal knocked over my glass, Marie! What a wizard he is, our Tadpole, to move so quickly that we could not even see him move!"

Dear little Maman, who in another moment must repair across the farmyard to the young count's kitchen, frowned more deeply than ever before, and once again attempted to speak seriously to Papa. "But I am worried, Michel-André. Can't you see that Pascal deserves his mother's worry? And his father's too?"

As for me, there I stood at the corner of the table, near my father's knee, my head and shoulders barely high enough to see the spot where the shattered glass had been, and grinning—foolishly I must admit—fully confused, totally proud of myself, and, in retrospect, savoring the shards of bright intensity that lit my wicked eyes in the same way that the unchanging sunlight lit the particles of Papa's *ballon* where they speckled the floor. I had no idea of what I had done or why, and yet I had fully intended to deprive Papa of his midday glass of wine and to destroy it. How curious to be so helplessly possessed of willpower.

"Michel-André," came the gentle sound of my mother's voice, "I think we should do something. . . ."

So they should have. My signs, as I have called them,

were warnings from another world which they might at least have attempted to heed, though no matter how much they had struggled with my occasionally distempered nature, it would have done no good. You can't straighten a crooked spoon, no matter how conscientiously you apply the polish.

And more such incidents first to be detected by the truly perceptive soul, of which even dear little Maman was not one, in that bright gleam in my eye? That fleeting sight of sheer unpredictability to others and purpose to me which even I could feel as the darkness that caused the faintest enlarging of my black eyes as my mood changed and some gloriously inappropriate act was all but mine? Of course there were. Uncountable. The day when Papa took me hunting, for instance, and instead of trudging behind him, aglow with the first incipient swellings of manhood, I merely stopped dead at his first shot and began to wail like a small child in the midst of emphatic punishment or some irrational denial. Of course had he been firing at a dove or quail, say, instead of at one of the great clumps of mistletoe that hung like beehives in the branches of the young count's poplars, things might have been different. And what of the late afternoon when the young count's wife discovered me alone with Maman in the château's vaulted kitchen and sent me into waves of agitation that caused that severely beautiful woman to taunt me and caused my mother to drop to her knees and hold me as if I were about to fly through the ceiling and so abandon them to grief and amazement forever. But that's too good a story to waste in a breath. It has its place in this narrative, which we'll find in time—with luck, that is, and patience, which even I am able to savor.

Let me now come directly to my affliction, since I have prepared well enough the bed of childhood devotion in which it lay curled as I myself lay curled in my own bed on all those spring nights when dear little Maman read to me of Armand the frog and when, at the conclusion of each such nightly episode, I then so generously allowed Maman to return to my father—more fool I, though I am tempted to add.

The good childhood exists only to welcome the worst of circumstances, as I have so often said, indirectly or not, and even my affliction, which was of a pitch and radiance to equal what Christophe suffered at the hands of his peculiar mother, brought to my life's beginning its own form of pleasure.

And how did it strike, that strange blow from which I could not recover yet without which I could not have lived? Quietly enough. It was simply that one day when I again took possession of the frog pond and lay attentively awaiting Armand's arrival, he did not appear. Not so much as a splash or even his oddly deformed head above the water. Nothing. The lily pad went empty; I tired of waiting for him or rather gave way to the most unpleasant kind of frustration that he could so abandon me. I lay on my stomach at the warm edge of the pond; I was filled with a kind of emptiness and hunger that I had not felt before. No bird of prey hovered overhead, not even the dragonflies disturbed the oily surface of the pond. Had something happened to Armand? Was his leathery body lying somewhere in the white grass immobile, already baking away to the last powdery remnants of his black hide? Or was he simply taking his ease on the bottom of the pond, half buried in succoring mud, dozing, somehow giving not the most fleeting thought to the child his mysterious ugliness had seduced to total dependency? Could he possibly be hiding himself away as deliberately as I was depriving Christophe of my visits? Was a frog capable of cruelty?

So the day went. The entire day. The result of that first day's fruitless vigil was that I frowned and pouted as never before, and Maman and Papa hardly dared to share a word between them, thanks to the prohibition of my dark mood. Why, that first night I was barely able to give myself over to the sights and sounds of the imaginary frog when Maman brought him to life with her soothing voice, thanks to the rage that I carried to bed with me because of the intolerable behavior of the frog that was real. And never to see the real Armand again? Or with the most dreadful infrequency and when I least expected him to show himself? Only in circumstances violently different from those provided by the frog pond itself? If I had known that first night that my overbearing frog was gone forever, at least in the ways I had known him, surely I would not have been able to go on but would have collapsed then and there, my only consolation being the feelings that would have overcome Maman and Papa at the sight of the shriveled skin left in my cold bed for them to discover.

Of course the shock of Armand's disappearance was gradual, which was why finally I was able to bear this change in my life until the day and hour when the dripping creature returned to me—in the form I could least have expected, which proved to be the heart of my affliction. And of course my determination to wait for him at the edge of the frog pond only grew with the passing of each empty day. I was not to be bested by a mere frog! I would survive his trickery, his malevolence, even his death if such was the answer to his absence. I would calm my rage, moisten my dry lips, force his return if only by the strength of my desire.

Then came the day and hour when, one afternoon in the midst of the many that so consumed me that I had long given up smiling or following Maman to the young count's kitchen and barely tolerated her nightly reading, something—an unfamiliar flash of color—caught my eye. I frowned more darkly, slowed my breath to a whisper, with the greatest possible stealth propped myself on my elbows and kept my eyes on the intrusive color. After a moment they came into sight. Two ducks! Two bright ducks floating side by side on a little stagnant pocket of water usually hidden from my view. Was this the answer? Had these passive birds, entirely foreign to my frog pond, frightened the missing frog into the murky depths of hiding? For a moment I felt relief, since if these ducks could terrify Armand, of course I could terrify the ducks. But then another soundless glance brought home the truth. Artificial! They were artificial! They were not even natural invaders of our frog pond! For in the moment I had seen that their colors were too bright to adorn living ducks, and that their heads did not turn, and that they made not a move against the listless muddy surface on which they sat. And how did these mere facsimiles of living ducks come to be floating so foolishly together on waters that belonged entirely to Armand and myself and the various kinds of plant growth they nourished? Papa! Papa, of course! For even as the bright paint continued to shine and sparkle on their wooden feathers, suddenly it came to me—those early evenings when I was on the verge of walking, but had not yet walked, and Papa used to sit carving his wooden ducks in front of the dying fire on the hot stones of our hearth. How heavy I must have been those evenings on my mother's lap, what a keen eye had my Papa, smoking his pipe and applying the blade of his knife against the blocks of wood destined to become in time those offensive ducks that were lifeless but not dead.

Dear little Papa, as I might have known! And in I plunged. I was determined to rid the frog pond of the mockery of those two ducks so innocently tethered by a string to the shore, for tethered they must have been, but in their mere presence destroying the integrity of the marshy place that was mine and wreaking who knew what havoc on my angry Armand. Of course I had no way of knowing the depth of the waters into which I flung myself and might well have sunk from sight then and there and drowned, as if in a cowardly effort to join Armand in the mud or in whatever entanglement of roots and weeds may have lain ready to entrap me beside my frog. But those waters, warm and gently putrid-smelling, as I noted in passing, swallowed me only to my thick chest, and forward I went, pushing, thrashing, fighting my way toward those wretched ducks. I stepped in holes, sank down, beat my babyish arms fruitlessly, in a veil of splashing progressed ever closer to those unwitting ducks.

Then I reached them, seized them, ripped them free of their tethers, and flung them to the embankment. Slowly, mouth half filled with water, I followed after them and pulled myself up that same embankment, where I stretched out panting beside the prickly bush inside which the green-and-white duck and the blue-and-white duck lay buried. Thus I promptly forgot what had driven me to such exertions, and rolled onto my back, allowed my mouth to hang slackly open, and fell into the deepest sleep I had ever known, exactly as if I had been subdued by Armand's spell in "The Stories of Armand the Frog," which was indeed the case, as I am now convinced.

Spell or no spell, that was the moment of my undoing, the turning point in my life. For suddenly I awoke gripped by pain as well as by the certainty of Armand's whereabouts and of what had happened to me in my dreamless sleep. I say dreamless, yet even now I remember the alien sensations that possessed me on the embankment—a pinching about my open mouth, a sudden ungentle filling of my mouth as with wet leathery fingers, a brief and useless period of dry heaving, and then the pain to which I awoke, doubled over on my side and gasping, thanks, I was convinced, to that treacherous frog, who had taken up his abode inside me, the very thought of which set me off again into still more painful spasms of regurgitation that produced nothing—no trickle of pond water, no signs of anything to be identified with Armand's body, no relief. Only the cramp that kept my knees to my chest as if I had been kicked in my poor little bloated stomach and, as I say, the certainty of what was causing my now stricken state. We must remember that until this day I had enjoyed nothing but the stalwart health of a two-year-old male child endowed with more than adequate weight and strength and doted upon by all those fortunate enough to have received him from the arms of a kind fate. Not so much as a cough, or the sting of a misguided bee. The very sunlight to little Christophe's sickly days. And now this.

Luckily for me, that pain in my otherwise wholesome stomach abruptly subsided when I heard Maman sweetly calling my name through the shadows that had begun to settle as I slept. Why, I even believe that I smiled when I felt myself suddenly relieved of pain and heard my dear little Maman calling. It came to me, I remember, that not every child is made to suffer the way I had just suffered, and would again and again my life long, and that it is not every small boy who bears inside him the secret that was now mine.

That evening I listened with new interest to one of

the episodes from "The Stories of Armand the Frog" and was spared any further abdominal attacks, though Maman did remark on the whiteness of my face—had the sun not changed my color even a shade?—and the wanness of my smile. Only some evenings later did my next attack occur, sending Maman and me early from dinner with Papa and up to my little bed, whose white sheets, I now recognized, had beckoned me all along not to healthy childhood but to affliction.

"Is he all right, Marie?" my father called anxiously from the foot of the stairs. "Oh, our poor Tadpole!"

"Don't fret, Michel-André," my mother called back down to him. "Tonight you must finish your meal alone."

"Just as you say, Marie," he answered in faintly wounded tones that made me realize clearly enough that he cared more about his stewed chicken than about my health or well-being, and that in fact he begrudged my mother's absence from his table. Here, then, and only a few nights after I had first been overcome by Armand, was something new. The understanding, that is, that as never before I now wanted Maman beside my bed and not below with my father, and that I myself wished to determine the length of each of her nightly vigils, and that any pain, but especially this one, was well worth my newfound gratification in denying Papa his pretty wife and causing him to eat his rapidly cooling dinner in silence. So there it was, Armand's double and apparently contradictory gift to me—dear little Maman and the abdominal ache now fierce, now fading, by which I inflicted myself, so to speak, on our household. Oh, that Armand was a clever fellow to intuit my deepest wishes and then to grant them by making me suffer as severely as he could in exchange.

"Pascal," my obviously worried mother whispered that evening, the third or fourth into my newly determined course of life, "perhaps you would prefer me not to read tonight?"

"No, Maman," I answered—yes, actually answered! For it was that very night that, holding my stomach and struggling to reveal no hint of the extent of my pain, I spoke my first words. "No, Maman, please read to me."

"But dear little Pascal," she whispered, "perhaps the pain will prevent you from listening. Perhaps you would prefer that I simply stroke your brow instead."

"No, Maman," I repeated, so softly that I well concealed the amazement I felt at my ability to speak, and to speak like an adult and not a child first stumbling into the sounds of speech. "I would like you to read to me, and not just one story tonight, but three. And Maman," I said as an afterthought, "I would like you to put your hand on my brow as well."

"Poor Pascal," she whispered, and did as I had asked.

And wouldn't you know, they were long stories and took most of the night to read, while she frowned gently and I lay propped on my back, my knees raised, my plump lower lip, worthy of any cherub's, I can tell you, caught between the two rows of my baby teeth. I kept my eyes on Maman, I felt the perspiration on the brow she kissed between each story that night. I listened, I saw on her face the expression of concern that was little more, it was plain to see, than a most attractive mask of the adoration of me that lay beneath, as if the greater her worry, the more blatant her love of her first and only child. It was a long night, with episode after episode of Armand's adventures drifting in and out of my awareness—how dreadful of that boy Henri to lop off one of the frog's small feet with his pocket knife!—and the horde of distant frogs filling the night with their now mournful song as if for my affliction and for the loss of their king, which the actual Armand had surely been. Only now and then did I find myself smelling the invisible orchard or the warm air as, half lost to sleep, I gave myself up to listening to Maman and watching the movement of her lips and, whenever I thought she would not notice, pressing into my stomach in the hopes that my fingers might discover the shape of the great frog within me and that I might nudge him and cause him to change his position, even to flatten himself and grow small, thus lessening my pain.

Once my father dared interrupt us.

"Marie," he called up from the foot of the stairs in a crude imitation of a stage whisper, his impatience fully evident both to Maman and to me, "haven't you spent long enough with him? Soon the entire night will be gone." Whereupon Maman paused, marked her place with a white finger, and tiptoed to the head of the stairs.

"Go to bed, Michel-André. I'll be down when I can."

"Our Tadpole is a marvel, Marie. But do come to bed."

At which I moaned, softly, even pleasantly, with just enough urgency not to alarm my mother unduly yet to bring her hastening back to me, as the darkness began to fade from the window behind her and one by one the voices of the far-off tiny frogs were extinguished. Shortly thereafter Armand must have slept as well, for my pain vanished and I slept as soundly as Armand, but not before I heard Maman descending the stairs. Had she turned her head and looked over her shoulder, she would have been pleased to see the faintest smile on the lips of her weary babe.

Of course the presence of the frog inside me resulted not merely in almost overpowering pain, which, in turn, was like a golden sauce enrobing the bliss of having dear little Maman all to myself those tranquil nights. For one thing, I began to fear for my diet and the effect it would have on Armand. I knew full well that ordinarily he ate insects of various kinds and algae and infinitesimal roots and sprouts that grew in the pond which he had forever denied himself. What now? I dismissed immediately the thought of attempting to eat what Armand had eaten before he had made his daring decision to abandon his pond for my stomach. And if he starved, slowly, until he died a miserable death in the darkness of my innermost source of life? He would not die peacefully, of that I was sure, and obviously would revenge himself in ways I could not imagine suffering, until at last he lay extinct within me—odious thought. It is one thing to carry within oneself a vital unruly frog, and quite another to have one's stomach uselessly burdened with a dead one. And if he died, obviously I would lose the clarity and power of pain, or its potential, that was now embedded in the pit of my stomach. At any rate I began to eat less, denied myself the sweet lamb and beef of Maman's famous roasts and stews—no more *boeuf en gelée* for me!—and subtly began to eat and hence feed Armand increasingly full bowls of shiny grain. But a more tormenting thought soon inflicted upon me a greater agony of confusion, even helplessness, which was nothing less than the fear of losing the very frog whose unwelcome presence I now so desperately entertained. To put it bluntly, I did all I could to restrain my babyish bowels, and every morning, after I had sat on my porcelain pot, in genuine dread I studied its contents, expecting on each occasion the sight of Armand paddling about my august chamber pot like a dying fish in a bowl. Gradually, however, those fears proved unnecessary, until my father and poor old Monsieur Remi, our village pharmacist, revived them in a burst of unwelcome medical effort. In the meanwhile, however, my sporadic cramps continued, for the most part during the night, accompanied by the sound of Maman's reading voice and the sound of the slowly turning pages. Why, many a morning I awoke to find her fully clothed and yet significantly disheveled, stretched out beside me, her head on my pillow, the essential storybook fallen closed between us, so increasingly diligent and exhausted was my Maman in her care of me, which was in fact nothing other than a mother's love sweetly spiced with a mother's worry.

The Frog

Need I remind you of "The Cook's Prayer"? How curious that I remember my father's crude song about my grandmother's teeth—all twenty-two of them—and yet am unable to bring to mind word for word, line for line, that prayer of my mother's. Perhaps it comes to me only in fragments because it belonged more in the mouth of an old woman than in my mother's. She could not have written it, of course, yet loved to recite it to me in the young count's kitchen. How did it go? Carnations decorating salmon and quail? And the fervent plea to cook the tongues of birds that have not yet ceased their singing? And aspics and frying sorbets? And finally the desire to use all her knowledge only to break a little bread at God's table? How touching it was that Maman should embody such artistry and so simple a heart!

I thought I knew Papa in the same way, assuming, for instance, that he was as much a victim of my frog as I was and, despite his puzzlement and downheartedness, would nonetheless offer no serious resistance to this newly established situation in which I had all but taken dear Maman away from him, since there is nothing in life like an ailing only child to split asunder the ordinary expectations of married life. How could he be any match for his suffering son and the power of an invisible frog? What could he do but accept his lonely place at the table and, throughout the most luxurious spring nights of his marriage to Maman—a thought I can hardly bear to allow to mind—take himself to his cold bed quite helpless to restore his wife to his side? Well, I was wrong, though he indeed managed to contain himself and preserve his guise of selfless submission to my apparently incurable condition for a remarkably long while, all things considered. In fact the air was already brisk and the harvesting in progress when, to my surprise, dear little Papa suddenly intruded once more between Maman and me. And how did he stop our nightly readings and bluntly recall his wife to himself? By using my own ill health as his ploy, which is to say that that man who pretended to good humor, to frankness and innocent vulgarity, the same person who in fact was so self-centered that one of my mother's "off days," as he called them, pitched him into the deepest gloom, finally reclaimed that dear woman simply by asserting himself on my behalf. Never, never would I have thought him quick-witted enough to conceive of such a transparent yet effective ruse!

"Marie," he said one night as she placed his large and steaming china plate before him—his napkin was already tucked into the top of his shirt—and as she prepared to ascend to my bedside, "these tribulations are intolerable. I am not speaking of mine, or yours and mine. I am a patient man. There is no more self-sacrificing mother than yourself. No, Marie, I am speaking of Pascal. Who knows what permanent disability his little internal organs may be suffering because of our good intentions? Who knows but what it is not already too late?"

At this my mother gave a little cry and—as I thought from the head of the stairs, where, in my nightshirt, I crouched and attempted to still my trembling and to quiet

Armand's swelling anger—must have paused and put her cool fingers to my father's unusually large mouth.

"Michel-André!" I heard her say in a frightened whisper. "Please! You must not say such things, my dearest!"

"For once it is my duty to speak out, Marie."

"But I am yours, Michel-André."

"I must tell you, then, that even a mother's love cannot replace the dictates of medical science! Soothing an internal malignancy may do more harm than good. Urgency of this sort requires treatment, not stories from a children's book! Otherwise . . . otherwise, Marie . . ."

"Hush, Michel-André. Please hush. I understand."

"Tomorrow, then, we shall take him to Monsieur Remi."

"Very well, my dearest."

Thus in a moment my father reestablished himself as provider, as protector, as male authority who stands before wife and child like the massive dead tree that glowers predictably and, if I may say so, stupidly over the living swamp. What a faker he was!

That night my pain was so intense that Maman abandoned entirely "The Stories of Armand the Frog," and simply joined me between my chilly sheets and lay comforting me the night long, until my own Armand, as anxious and angry as I was myself, at last succumbed to her caresses. Soon enough I followed suit.

Generally the prospect of a visit to Monsieur Remi, who not only was the pharmacist in the village nearest the Domaine Ardente but was he who acted as our local dental surgeon and medical practitioner as well, roused in me the happiest of expectations. His pharmacy was a small boy's delight, a dark comforting place smelling of pills and powders, capsules and heavy bottles of black liquid, and divided in half by a partition of hand-rubbed mahogany that rose from the tiled floor almost to the ceiling. This ancient wooden wall, behind which Monsieur Remi and his assistant worked, was covered with mysterious examples of the woodcarver's art, elaborate scrolls and highly polished flourishes. In wooden niches sat large jars of white and yellow porcelain, clearly labeled to indicate their contents. And the old pair of scales of brass and iron, what a marvelous machine it was, with its gears and little row of weights so simple yet complex that as a mechanism it was the perfect counterpart to the great clock in the corner, the one—the pair of scales—stock-still yet always ready to lend itself to the precise measurement of Monsieur Remi's curatives, the other—the clock—also rooted in stillness yet housing its long pendulum, whose steady swing and loud ticking made monotonous the very idea of motion. No matter the troop of ailing citizens who always stood on file in Monsieur Remi's pharmacy, shifting uncomfortably in a place so clean and speaking grandly of matters beyond their ken, daunted, the lot of them, with heads hanging like children ashamed of their rashes or broken bones or bowel troubles, waiting their turn at the counter like the bank teller's window in our old bank, behind which stood our benevolent man of healing, Monsieur Remi; never was I repelled by the inevitable shabbiness of sickness, and never did I consider the pharmacy a refuge for the sick and injured, but merely assumed that it was a central landmark of my childhood and intended for my own pleasure and little more. After all, never was I one of those who entered the pharmacy with some kind of medical complaint, large or small, since during our infrequent visits to Monsieur Remi I acted only as my mother's companion, and certainly she bore no resemblance to the other villagers seeking his help and kindness.

In those days the pharmacist was as important to that little village as the priest himself, and his place of work as timeless and central to the village as the dark and ugly church to which most people flocked on Sundays. Luckily for me, the young count and his wife tolerated the pharmacy but not the church, so of course my parents, unlike the rest of those on the Domaine Ardente, followed suit. Why "luckily for me"? Simply, I suppose, because I was not a child born to learn anything or to submit to the cold interests of a man dressed in black skirts and a madly flapping black hat. At any rate I loved our local pharmacy, as I have said. Furthermore, a trip to the village always promised not only my chance to stare about me at the marvels stored in gleaming vials and dangerous-looking boxes, and to watch my dear mother as, in all her prettiness, she leaned forward and held her whispered conference with Monsieur Remi, that smiling old man in high collar and white apron; it also promised a ride in the young count's mighty Citroën.

What a stately machine it was, long and high, the only

automobile for kilometers around, a great glistening creature brightly lacquered a soft beige that was the color of one of the crepe-de-chine flouncy feminine garments belonging to the young count's wife, and trimmed with dark chocolate-colored bands. Yes, it was in this auto and driven by Papa himself, who sat in front with his head up and chin thrust out, and with his arms extended horizontally and stretched to their fullest so that both his hands could grip the steering wheel, that my mother and I made our trips to the village, snuggling proudly together in the back seat, happily smelling the warm leather and the fumes from the engine. Pharmacy and lavish automobile, what a kindred pair they were! And how generous was the young count, to loan his auto to Papa for our family needs.

But on the day of which I speak, when Papa was attempting to relieve me of pain and hence wreak who knows what havoc on the frog who was mine and entirely unknown to the rest of the world, ours was not a happy family that climbed into the Citroën and set off for the village. Initially the engine refused to start for my grim, preoccupied father. Maman held my hand without the slightest enthusiasm. A fat duck barely escaped being the victim of our assembled gloom. And what do you think, the village priest was hosting a funeral when we drove into the village square and parked so heavily and darkly in front of the pharmacy that we quite overshadowed the old horse-drawn hearse drawn up before the church. Only later did we learn that it had been kindly Monsieur Remi himself who had sold little Christophe's mother the rat poison, though after all, what might we have expected?

Melodrama? Why not? In those days the pharmacist worked hand in hand with the village priest, though the two refused to speak to each other. And who but our own countrymen are the sort to misuse lonesome public urinals shaped like upended coffins and made of porcelain at that? After all, indiscretion is only the flowering of desperation. It just shows how light of heart we are.

But to return to the church, the pharmacy, and the Citroën that was already stealing the crowd's attention from the horse and hearse and the coffin just nosing its way from between the church portals as the bell began its tolling. There we were, Papa exactly as he had been since the start of our journey, stern and silent in the front seat, and I alone in the rear, unnecessarily holding my stomach and dreading the return of Maman and its aftermath. The interior of the young count's auto was vast and impersonal, thanks to its scent of leather and fuel and all the hidden machinery by which it worked. Yet despite his pride and autocratic pose at the wheel, Papa could not help introducing into this regal atmosphere the faint barnyard smells for which he was famous and of which he could not rid his person, for all his scrubbing. It was fitting, somehow, that the young count's occasional chauffeur should smell of hens and cow manure.

Maman returned. Slowly and in a formal, distracted fashion, Papa quit our vehicle to assist Maman, who was carrying several parcels wrapped in white paper and returning to me and taking her place at my side. How white she was and serious, despite her weak smile.

"And have you met with success, Marie?" he said. "I thought you would."

Again the village reverberated to the rhythms of our enormous engine coming to life. And off we drove in an easterly direction toward the Domaine Ardente, while the hearse proceeded toward the west, of course, and its bleak destination of old monuments and photographs of the precious dead. Could it have been anything other than our distinctive fate that caused the burial of little Christophe's father on the very day that my own father attacked my frog, using my mother as his sham agent of mercy? Surely not. And perhaps little Christophe was luckier than I in the long run; who knows? At least his father had a shorter life than mine.

No sooner had Papa opened the auto door for my package-laden mother than he stepped aside, still secretly enjoying the import of the occasion, frowning and raising his black brows, while she, stooping, spilled her packages, seized me round the waist, and, laughing and reverting to her usual optimistic mood, drew me into her girlish, motherly-smelling embrace, leaving Papa to retrieve the packages.

"Marie," he said, after he had disposed of them on our scarred and oily kitchen table, or perhaps into my mother's arms again—does it matter?—and retreated hastily to the open door, "I don't believe that I can remain in the house while you minister to our little Tadpole. You know that I cannot bear his pain or yours. You know my inclination to nausea, my love."

"Dear Michel-André," she said with a laugh, her color returning along with her usual energy and quickness, "you are just too sensitive. So take a walk, my dear. We will not be long."

Thus we were alone at last, dear little Maman and I, on the brink of something deeply personal, as I intuited, and in the daylight hours as well. My foreboding increased proportionally with my pleasure or with the pleasure dear little Maman appeared to anticipate. With reassuring eagerness she gathered up whole armfuls of fluffy white towels—more than even she knew were stored in her various chests or on her shelves—and set a pot to warming. Actually, she knelt beside me to unwrap the packages so that we might consider together the length of supple hose, the fat glass bottle, the funnel, the corks and clamps, and the carton of sweet-smelling salts, all provided by our kind and trusty Monsieur Remi. What must she have been thinking when she listened, nodding, to the old man's instructions!

Grudgingly—perhaps warily is the more fitting word —I climbed the stairs to my now sunlit room, my handsome chamber pot, which Maman had said we would not need, nonetheless swelling ever larger inside my head, its water swishing about and the weight of it, though it still remained hidden behind the pretty flowered curtain of my bedside stand, more laden than ever with the shocking fate it promised Armand and me. How could I preserve Armand's security and yet submit to Maman's rite of cleansing, no matter how free of discomfort she assured me it would prove, and so rapidly over? Even then I did not entirely understand what was in the offing for Armand and me, or at least initially for me, but I knew that the conflict it posed was without resolution.

In this instance Maman was wrong, for her efforts to follow Monsieur Remi's instructions were not at all brought rapidly to a conclusion. In fact the further along she went, the longer the process took. But at the same time, the more towels she spread or heaped on my turned-down bed, beside which I stood watching and waiting, clothed only in my nightshirt, and hence feeling inappropriately nude, given the time of day, and the more engrossed she became in testing the water in the kettle she had brought up from the kitchen, or flexing the white tube and struggling to make use of the various clamps by trial and error, or smelling the contents of this carton or that, and surveying the scene and smoothing the white apron she had donned for the occasion, the less time mattered and the more I submitted now to foreboding, now to agreeable expectation, slowly tipping this way and that as did the brass dishes of Monsieur Remi's scales. The sunlight bore down upon my bed, focusing on our little amphitheater, as it were, an illumination and a warmth that would never fade. As for my mother, the more she became engrossed in the procedure she clearly intended to master and carry through to its end, the more girlish and pleased with herself she became, as if she were once again the young girl giggling over her trousseau and the immediate prospects to come.

"You see, darling," she said, more to herself than to me, "it is all quite simple and painless. No one, not even Monsieur Remi's assistant, could undertake this ordinarily distasteful business with any more tenderness than your Maman. Trust me, my little Tadpole. Trust your Maman!"

In many ways she was quite correct, and her girlish absorption in what she meant to do to me was quite justified. How could I not climb to my bed as she asked? How could I not readily lie on my stomach, attempting not to press my full weight on Armand, of course, and how not give myself up to the thick, soft surface of the towels and the sunlight that warmed me when, with another almost inaudible sound of suppressed giggling, she drew up the hem of my nightshirt, at once dispelling my fright by the warm feathery touch of her fingers. Somewhere between her emergence from the pharmacy and her entrance into our farmhouse, brimming that day with the smell of her garlic soup, she had lost her fear of having to inflict something so foreign on her only son, and so potentially filled with tension and tears, which is the kindest way of putting it, and had regained her usual energy and sweetness, the will of the competent mother who is more than content to perform such odious chores by allowing to the fore the power of the young bride's desire and anxiety. *Thy Weakness Is Thy Strength*, as I have heard it said!

Just as she promised, it mattered not at all that from time to time she lost control of the coil of hose and sprayed warm water everywhere. And when she slipped and the water splashed and trickled down my inner thighs or even my rugged little calves, why, it was not an unpleasant sensation at all, quite the opposite, while the water disappeared almost at once into my bed of absorbent towels and Maman managed to stroke and at the same time playfully pinch my buttocks, no doubt to distract me from what was happening. My broad smile, half buried in my pillow, was the perfect match for her giggling or those long silent moments when she held her breath in concentration and the hose slid forward—or upward, inward, whatever you please—accompanied by the hurtful swelling that must have given Armand no end of surprise, since for once he was not the cause of my delicious pain.

Did poor Christophe's mother treat him in this fashion? Obviously not. And what of those children in public sickbeds and tended only by old women who scorned their wards and, once a day, by lone men in long beards and long coats who were but waiting their chance to leave those sickly children and seize their bouquets and hurry off to their midday meals with ladies in large hats? And what about dear little Papa, striding anxiously and angrily back and forth in a chilly glen, while I lay half naked in the house he had fled, basking beneath warm sun and dear little Maman's full attention and timid hands? What perfection!

Yet all this while my reluctance lay in reserve like the

very Armand I could not bear Maman to disturb where he lay in darkest uncertainty. I condoned Maman's exploration of that second most private area of my chubby body, condoned her fingers and sparkling eyes on my softest flesh, which I myself would never see. I even admitted the slippery tips of her fingers to make me startle and laugh outright, and the slippery tip of the rubber hose to achieve, as I have said, its still further penetration. And as I have also said, I accepted, even welcomed, the sensation of the warm water swelling within me. But only so much. Only as much as I thought Armand, who had chosen me above an entire pond of warm water, after all, would permit. So throughout it all my readiness to refuse the will and hand of Maman was at the ready. One drop too much for my defenseless frog, the drop that would plunge us both into the roiling waters that could only end in catastrophe and ugliness, and I would exert myself even against my own dear little Maman. I was thus prepared as much for her sake as for my own and Armand's. Even she, strong person that she was, would never have recovered from the sight of Armand expelled half drowned and thoroughly battered onto my fluffy towels. No, I would prevent such a disaster, beyond a doubt.

"Stop, Maman!" I cried at the last possible moment, and so forcefully that she was indeed able to staunch the potential flooding with her poor, suddenly rigid fingers.

"But darling, what's the matter? We have only a little more to finish. Let yourself go, my dearest. Please. Do what Maman asks."

"No, Maman," I said firmly, clutching myself against the waters.

"But I must, Pascal."

Was I not as helpless under the bare hands of my mother as the fictional Armand once was when cupped in the cruel hands of Henri? I was. How terrible, then, my dilemma, for in fact I had no choice but to obey Maman, yet could not. I could not reveal to anyone in the world, even to Maman, the reason why I must deny any such further tampering with my internal self, but must instead guard my body, undeveloped as it was, with my very life. To reveal my secret would have branded me forever with an odious stigma—that of derangement—so undeserved and degrading that beneath it I would have been crushed to extinction. So too Armand. Yet what choice did I have? Whereupon and suddenly I determined that to my loving mother I could only hazard the truth. She at least would believe me.

"Maman," I whispered, "there is a frog inside me."

She paused. She said nothing. I felt one of her cool hands flat on my lower back, I felt the fingers of her other hand pinching tight the clamp that closed off the tube. Then slowly she withdrew the tube and emptied it into the kettle, while the toweling beneath me grew hot and wet, then merely damp and warm.

"Pascal," she said in her softest, most serious voice, "you know that what you have just said is impossible."

"No, Maman," I answered without moving, "it's not."

"Then you dreamt this frog? Isn't he really the little

66

magical creature from 'The Stories of Armand the Frog'?"

"No, Maman, he's not. Though his name is Armand."

"A real frog, then, my child?"

"Yes, Maman."

There was another and longer pause. Papa clenched his fists and lips in the dark wood. Maman, my lovely nurse and physician both, considered our dilemma. Finally she spoke, still in her most worried tones.

"What are we to do, Pascal?" she asked.

"I shall find ways to appease Armand, Maman. I shall control my cramps. I shall require less of your time at night. Papa will consider me cured. He will be happy once more, Maman. You'll see."

Again she paused, and now I was aware of her mood reversing its course and of our morning together drawing to its gentle close, which pleased me though already I knew that dear little Maman was slipping away from me as, reluctantly, she drew down the gathered bottom of my nightshirt. I distinctly thought that she would have enjoyed playing awhile longer with the hose, the lubricant, the purgatives, and my plump nudeness, or occasionally repeating mornings like this one. As for me, I might have remained forever spread-eagled for Maman, if I had not had to save Armand from the loosened waters.

"Very well, my dearest," she murmured then. "Papa would not mind our little well-meant deception. Because we love him."

At that very moment my father returned to us and, from the foot of the stairs and feebly overcoming his hesitation, called up to us, inquiring as to the state of completion and degree of success of what my Maman had undertaken, whereupon and in her liveliest voice she affirmed her achievement of all he had hoped for. She even carried down to him my heavy, shining chamber pot, though she refused to lift aside its flowered cloth and insisted on emptying and refilling it herself. My father said that his Marie was a marvel, which was how he spoke when he wished most to shower upon my dear mother his highest words of commendation.

How's that? My frog merely a figment concocted from imaginary vapors for the sake of a personality forever in the sway of infantile desires? Oh, there's an unworthy thought. But I am the first to admit that from the time I first fell into my profound sleep beside the frog pond until I was rushed to the room above Monsieur Remi's pharmacy—that room in which he practiced his crude forms of dentistry—I had no actual proof that I had in fact swallowed a frog. But seeing is believing, as they say. And we shall see. Of course the young count's wife shared the world's skepticism, as she made manifestly clear a few days following the incident I have just described. In later life I have often thought that it was Papa himself who wanted to give me that enema which, thank God, he was forced to entrust to dear little Maman, thanks to your generally accepted rules of convention. What a brutal business it would otherwise have been! *Mon Dieu!* But you see that I am not always ready to do mighty battle with convention. Far from it. Many a moment of safety and well-being I owe to convention. After all, I am not so different from anyone else, if the truth be known.

But speaking of truth, the young count's wife was one of my first accusers, confronting me when I was still recovering from the silent intimacy that Maman and I had shared and from what I had been forced to promise her on Papa's account. I have already spoken of the signs which, had they been properly read, would have indicated beyond a doubt the road my life had already chosen from childhood to old age—though I am still a young man, despite how I may appear to the world at large. Certainly I was attractive enough to the young count's wife, no matter how unjustly she accused me as a consequence. The voluptuary appears in many guises, as you and I know full well, and as I learned in my earliest days of accommodating myself to Armand the frog. As for "signs," what a day for "signs" that was! Why, they were a veritable bombardment, and I such a young and innocent voluptuary to fall into the hands of that unappeasable young woman.

Loss of consciousness without loss of motor locomotion—there we have it, one of the minor but sometimes embarrassing or even frightening indispositions clustered around my invisible burden like gems in a crown. Hardly had I swallowed my glorious yet malicious frog than I became an occasional sleepwalker in daylight hours. It was not a pleasant experience, to come awake, so to speak, in unfamiliar surroundings, completely lost, or worse still to find oneself an unwitting trespasser in forbidden realms, such as that luckily empty room with *Mes-*

dames written in curlicues on the door and where once I was discovered by an amused lady dressed in black. Such women are not all so well disposed, I can tell you.

Well, yes, my one and only confrontation with the young count's wife was not dissimilar, at least at the outset. There I was, suddenly come to myself without the slightest recollection of where I had been or how I happened to be where I was, deep within the young count's château, which I recognized in the instant that I recognized myself in abrupt and awful wakefulness. The white walls, the tiled floors, a hanging tapestry depicting a wounded stag on the run, a distant chandelier, all were as familiar and horrifying as if I had in fact seen them before, which I had not. And why did I stand so firmly where I stood, a small child uninvited, certainly, and unwanted according to anyone's ordinary assumptions?

Because not only had I somehow invaded the interior of the young count's château, as even my Maman had never done, but also—Heaven forbid!—I was standing as if turned to wood directly in the doorway of the boudoir—there was only one!—belonging to the young count's wife. And she was within! Precisely as ordained by my treacherous frog and that insistent scheme of all things to come, at least as far as I was concerned, that young and formidable woman lay stretched out before me in a half-sitting position on a chaise longue covered in rose-colored chintz on which large but faded roses glowed in the sunlight. How odd I must have looked to her, a chubby male child who could not have been more unexpected or more comical, with his mouth agape, his little fists clenched, his small eyes growing larger and rounder by the moment.

How close she was! And if I was an amusing sight to her—her own cook's son and frightened out of his wits —how wondrous she looked to me, wearing as she did a peignoir of beige crepe de chine and silk stockings. She was smiling, I saw the moist webbing where her lips joined at their corners, the peignoir had fallen open here and there as if it had a languorous mind of its own. Larger and larger she loomed, with a strand of auburn hair come loose and flashing independently in the sunshine. Perhaps she thought I was a God-sent diversion, whereas what she saw on my face was not only a paralysis of sight—indeed it was that, since I could not tear my eyes from her—but also a reflection of the frog-inflicted suffering that I owed to Armand at that moment. What a time to unleash his attack on my stomach, when for the first time my eyes were attacking me with desire, so that I could not tell the one from the other, pain from desire, desire from pain. At any rate her stockings were the color of dark chocolate smeared on the tips of a woman's fingers, while the legs they covered grew in proportion to the increasing immensity of the young count's wife and the width of her smile, as if the chaise had become an ornate boat dwarfed, in a sense, by the ever approaching woman riding its stern. But oh, what that woman did then, which even now sets me to trembling with both anger and desire. Would you believe it? She tempted me! For no sooner had she realized what a serious captive I was than she raised one of those stockinged legs of hers. Yes, raised it! At the knee! Encircling the top of her exposed thigh with her bejeweled hands, slowly she raised into full view a dark, sculpted knee, and then slowly she stiffened that entire leg and raised it at a low and precious angle so that the satin garter straps were revealed for only me to see. And, with her eyes fixed on mine and her smile suddenly frozen on her superbly oiled face, was she not, intentionally and unintentionally as well, smoothing the stocking on that one broad thigh? She was! She was! And the rings and gems adorning the fingers of those wicked hands flashed their keen message directly into my small face like an explosion.

One thought came to me. Namely, that Maman's garters were white, not flesh-colored, at which my ears filled with a terrible sound, the overwhelming clacking sound of my own small boots, and my chest filled with a terrible breathlessness. My boots were like small blocks of wood on the tiles, and up and down they went until they carried me off in full flight, and just in time. Oh, I was too young a child, I understood, to smile at the young count's wife, to speak to her, to step into her forbidden chamber. So what other choice did I have, except to spurn the young count's wife and to flee?

Flee I did, this way and that, darting hither and thither up further wide flights of stairs and down, pursued by my own veritable racket through labyrinthine corridors and into rooms I had not seen before—fortunately I bumped into nothing, broke nothing—and wheeled and flew on with my short arms outspread, my body bent double, as if I had turned into poor little Christophe himself.

Lost? Indeed I was as hopelessly displaced as any child who cannot find his way in a dark wood, when—exactly —all at once I emerged into that dear room I knew so well—my own mother's kitchen in the young count's château, of course—and clattered abruptly to a halt, safe at last. The great black stove, as large as one of our then primitive locomotives, was alight with heat, around the walls the brass and copper pots hung like suits of armor, and on the massive table, dark and oiled with my mother's years of artistry, there rested a snow-white steaming platter, waiting to be carried off to its place before its expectant diners. The blue and yellow tiles gleamed around the enormous sink, water trickled from a spout whose mouth was as large as mine, an iron lid danced on its agitated pot on the stove. And yet that warm and savory kitchen was empty. Where was my mother in her white apron and holding aloft a wooden spoon?

As quietly as I could I approached the table, drawn like our abandoned child to a wisp of smoke rising through the black-and-white trees, and as quietly drew out a wooden chair and pulled myself to a kneeling position on its rattan seat. Whereupon I did not smile, losing myself in what I saw, or sniff like the immense rabbit blindly following the scent of our frightened child, or reach out my pudgy forefinger and dip it into the creamy heat in which this roast or that usually filled the platter too hot to touch, as I often did, but quite the opposite. Oh, I drew back and sat bolt upright, as mortified by what I saw heaped on the platter as I had been by the substantial silken thigh with which I had been confronted only moments before.

Frogs' legs! Yes, frogs' legs! Who could possibly believe such a crude and hurtful coincidence, such a blatant blow to the already scattered senses of a child so young of age? And how did all those nearly translucent halves of frogs, which were like nothing so much as the swiftly sautéed bodies of tiny men lopped in half at the waist, come to be piled hot and ready on that white platter? Papa, of course! Who else could have plundered my frog ponds, sloshing around in the cold mud as happily as he had shattered the clumps of mistletoe from the bare limbs of the silvery poplars—who else could have amassed so many poor frogs as a special gift for the young count's table? Papa, I say. Who else? Oh, it is true that I could not help but be agreeably touched by Maman's use of garlic and olive oil in her preparation of all my slaughtered frogs, though there in the presence of so many butchered carcasses I could hardly hold back my tears, my cries of anger, or the convulsions that threatened to expel the mighty Armand, in which case how awful the sight that would have met his bulging stare, and how pathetic my poor frog's croaking.

At least it did not come to that. For just as I thought that I could bear no more, unable to defeat my incipient nausea or the trembling that was already threatening to assume complete control of me from head to foot, dear Maman came to my rescue, as she always did, sweeping me off my chair and into her warm and flour-scented arms.

"Pascal!" she cried softly, hugging me against the dragons she was unable to see yet knew had somehow emerged from the corners of this wholesome room, this workshop devoted to health and good taste, and were slithering toward me. Little could she fathom what I had already suffered, though in an instant more she was to see for herself an example of the dark forces with which I so bravely, and sometimes joyously, struggled. "My poor Pascal," she whispered. "I did not even know you were here. . . ."

"Oh yes," came an answering voice—that of the young count's wife, naturally. "He is indeed here, Marie!"

"Madame . . . !" said my dear little Maman, looking up in surprise and unintentionally releasing me, and smiling. "Madame . . . ?"

I stared, and Maman wilted into the depths of her sweet nature, for there before us, as I have just indicated, stood the young count's wife, the very image of beauty who had nonetheless appeared soundlessly, all at once, and contradictorily, so to speak, on the wings of stealth, exactly as I had appeared to her, except that I had done so without volition.

In the short time since I had fled her boudoir, she had apparently gone through one of those purely feminine rituals that should have taken half the day, for she had discarded her peignoir of gloriously beige-colored crepe de chine and in its place donned a mauve-colored gown, or rather a gown of layer upon layer of gauzy chintz, one pale yellow, another the color of the faded rose, then back to a pale bluish purple that was, if anything, more enticing than the soft blessed beige of the peignoir intended only for the young count's eyes. Why, her entire present garment appeared transparent, and yet was not. She might have been dressed only in a colony of the first butterflies of spring or the last of fall, though it was impossible to catch the slightest sign of the half-corset that held her fleshiness firmly into the hourglass shape so desirable in those days. Her amber-colored hair was swept up and partially formed into a large chignon, her skin was tighter and shinier than ever, her invisible legs in their silky satin were undeniable. Not smiling, or not exactly smiling, she was towering close to me, and looking down on me. I could smell her. There was no garlic in the world that could compete with that woman's smell, which was not entirely of perfume, as I can attest.

"Well, Marie, are you not ashamed to have such a boy as this for a son?"

"Madame!" cried Maman, quite forgetting her place, as the expression went. "Whatever do you mean?"

"This boy is devious, Marie. He is not to be trusted."

"Pascal? Oh, you have never spoken this way before, Madame."

"He lies!" responded the young count's wife, though in a soft and powdery voice. "He cannot tell the truth, Marie!"

Poor dear Maman was on the verge of tears, she who was as young as the woman accusing her so inexplicably, and far prettier, thanks to her sweetness of soul and her cooking. I too felt my small eyes brimming, and my head swirling in the face of magnificence draped, as it were, in cruel senselessness, just as the compacted flesh gave resting place to such a myriad of fluttering butterflies, as might a tree trunk or some lithesome bush.

"There is something wrong with him!" insisted that regal young woman flatly, which must have struck home and caused dear Maman to believe that her mistress, ordinarily not at all a lofty or judgmental woman, had somehow divined Maman's burden and the secret she and I had agreed to share and, above all, to preserve. So now, in an instant, I was assaulted not only by the guilt that rightly belonged to my accuser but also by a still deadlier fear—namely, that my mother would not be able to remain faithful to me and to our secret. As indeed she could not.

"Oh, Madame," she said then, in a broken whisper. "My poor little Pascal . . . Oh, my poor son . . . he believes that there is . . . that he suffers from having . . . Oh, Madame, my little Pascal thinks that he has a frog in his stomach!" This last she finally revealed with hanging head and in a voice all but inaudible.

There it was. My secret was out. And no penitent in a confessional could have unburdened herself more pathetically than did my Maman that afternoon. My ears flamed, my small dark hostile eyes were awash. How foolish my secret sounded when spoken aloud in the light of day—my mother's "thinks" had not been lost on me—how great the suffering I had inflicted upon dear sweet Maman.

It was at this point precisely that the young count's wife, succumbing to the heat of my mother's kitchen, as Maman herself never did, unless in the throes of some final preparation, which this was not, showed me the wet light of her broad forehead and beckoned me with her parted lips and the tip of her tongue, and all at once stepped forward to embrace, not me—as understandably I had expected—but dear Maman. Beyond a doubt the young comtesse drew close to my Maman and embraced her, and thrust her mouth all but into the depths of Maman's dark curly hair. So the full mouth fell upon the precious ear—to devour it? Or merely to whisper into it, mistress of a château stooping to confide to that château's chef as ordinary women are wont to do, but not mistress and cook. And never shall I forget those whispered words. *I can tell you worse, Marie!* There, exactly, is what the young Comtesse de Beauval whispered to my own Maman that day. *I can tell you worse, Marie!*

Whereupon, and though I was helpless to do so, I fled, or rather did my best to flee, which is to say that as if to drown out those words and those that must follow in her next warm breath, my ears were again filled with the clacking of my tightly laced little boots. Like wood, blocks of wood. Like ranks of drummers beating upon skulls with wooden sticks.

At any rate it was a deafening racket, as up and down pounded my fat knees, shaking my clenched teeth, my fists, the wet cowlick on my brow. How I danced in my blind flight to nowhere. Then the young count's wife spoke aloud, in a clear voice and not as unkindly as I imagined that afternoon.

"But there is certainly something wrong with him, Marie. Epilepsy, perhaps. Yes, I think it is epilepsy."

Here I must insist that I danced and shook as I did, forcing poor Maman to gasp and throw her arms about me and attempt to still my by now drenched gyrations in the folds of her skirts, because I feared that the young comtesse would recount to my mother how I not only had appeared in her boudoir like an apparition of earliest possible lust in a child but by doing so had made the comtesse my own poor mother's rival! No wonder I danced my way to oblivion that day. And what a nasty bit of trickery it was, for never, never did my mother have a rival for my affection!

When I returned to consciousness I could not have been more relieved to find myself in my own white bed and not on some brocaded couch in the château, and tended by my Maman and not by the young comtesse, though a faint smell of her still lingered. At least I have given that woman her due, as promised. I must admit that her proud stockinged leg retains a special place in my memory, where it can no longer cause my dear Maman any harm. And perhaps it was offered to me all those years ago in unsuspecting naturalness. Who knows?

The frogs' legs? Why, I have always had an aversion to frogs' legs, and still do, recognized the world round though that sumptuous dish may be as a symbol—a flagrant symbol, as everyone knows—of our national cuisine. Emotions aside, the very presence of Armand the frog denies me the role of Pascal the cannibal. My own fare is still simple, despite my unusual gifts as a chef and except for carefully rationed moments of self-indulgence. Like mother, like son, as the saying goes. And no, the leg of the young count's wife is not the flesh I have promised. I can do better by our unfettered flesh than that stockinged leg, I can tell you!

Proof, you say? Proof positive of Armand's existence? So we're back to that, are we? A gentle reminder? I'm grateful for it. I do not enjoy being knocked about by scoffing and mocking. However, *Exceptional is he who hosts the frog,* which I would ask you to remember, if you will. It was whispered by Armand the frog to little Vivonne one day when she lay asleep by the cool brook. But it might as well be shouted from the housetops, that majestic pronouncement, proof or no proof. As for scoffing and mocking, let me be reasonable and admit again that no one enjoys encountering at every turn the disbelieving grin, the

cocked eyebrow, the face pursed to the tones of contradiction, inevitably to be the butt of humiliation, disagree-
ment, dismissal, silence, the turned fat back of the egoist
who attempts, by feigned indifference, to obliterate one's
very existence from the gathering. In certain respects, as I
say, I am like every man. How then do I stand apart?
Well, I have had my lifetime of suffering, inflicted upon
me merely because of talking too much, talking too fast,
too often discovered lost, too much weeping in public or
laughing long and loud at what the public at large deems
offensive. Is a little sleeplessness and fist pounding so very
out of the way? While we're on this subject, what gave
the young count's wife the right to make the diagnosis she
did that afternoon in the overheated place of my mother's
artistry, and hence heap upon my poor Maman an additional worry from which that dear woman was never entirely freed and which, like the back of a hand, swept my
own dear mother off to her grave, or helped to? The young
count's wife was wrong, you see. To this day there is not
a person alive, not even one of those men, young and old,
who make their daily rounds in Saint-Mamès, who is able
to find a diagnostic term for what afflicts me. It is certain,
however, that the young count's wife was off the mark. I
am anything but an epileptic. And of course the physicians
of Saint-Mamès know nothing at all about the true Armand. And if they did? Oh, what a lot of sorry faces at
finding all their learning and all their healing powers given
the lie by a mere frog! What bafflement! What oblitera-
tion! The joke is always on the physician, not on the poor

fool given unto his care. *Exceptional is he who hosts the frog!*

Oh, very well. Very well. Proof positive. No more procrastination. There is no excuse for it, since what I have to tell is more amazing than anything a young dancing woman attempting to entertain an entire regiment of amputees can pull from her hat.

It began one break of day when I awoke screaming, not, as we might expect, from pain attributable to that malicious frog of mine, not in the abdomen, that is, but from a stabbing pain in one of my small white teeth. Not a bellyache, this time, but a toothache, and one so strong and so different from what I had so far experienced that in consuming my entire mouth and my entire lot of early teeth it quite cloaked the true culprit in anonymity. Here was a new demon, from which even Armand cowered.

Maman rushed to my aid, of course, while Papa took up his usual place at the foot of the stairs, no doubt white of face and mindlessly stuffing what he could of his nightshirt into his trousers. Again there was the young count's Citroën, though this time brightly frosted over with the cold air of that early dawn. Again there was the long journey down country roads empty except for the occasional hailing farmer, to whom my distraught father did not wave back. Again the pharmacy, though it was closed, until dear Maman returned to us accompanied by the sleepy, half-dressed Solange, Monsieur Remi's assistant, and bearing the news that Monsieur Remi was spending two days and nights, as luck would have it, with his sister in the neighboring village of La Flêche. There was not time, said Maman, to drive to La Flêche and back again, and so I was to be in the care of Solange, that irritable young woman whose reluctance to speak and whose face, disfigured with prettiness, as Papa liked to say in his best moods, made her appear more appropriate to the farmyard than to the pharmacy. However, and as quickly as we could, Maman and I followed Solange to a side door, waited as patiently as we could while Solange, like an indifferent jailer, grappled with a great ring of keys and my wailing roused a nearby dog and Maman urged Solange to hurry. That young woman, who was obviously immune to my wailing, to Maman's anguish, and to the barking of the angry dog, finally led us up narrow stairs and into a small room, where poor Maman was instructed to wait behind a closed door, lone occupier of the room's lone chair, and I, holding my face in the typical gesture of a child's first and hence unimaginable toothache, was left to follow Solange into Monsieur Remi's workplace of dental healing. For a moment, and even in the half-light admitted to us by the shutters, which it took Solange a long, thoughtless time to open, I quite forgot my agony. I saw that this room, befitting Monsieur Remi's efforts to pit himself against pain like mine, or to fashion new teeth, if such they could be called, for rustics still living in the country roundabout this village, was as magical as Maman's kitchen occupying its place of honor in the young count's château. Despite the poor light, I saw arranged in rows like toy soldiers whole ranks of instruments with ivory handles and, on porcelain blocks somewhat larger than a man's mouth, seat of aching or missing teeth, innumerable sets of artificial teeth awaiting installation, no matter the resistance of him into whose sad mouth such ill-fitting teeth were jammed. Around the dismal walls were benches shining impossibly with bright blades, creatures that looked like pliers intended for automotive repair, and tools large and small for fashioning new instruments to replace those that broke or simply disintegrated, as they did in time. This place, the pride and joy of Monsieur Remi, was much like a museum created especially to delight the child, the male child, since much of its equipment and many of the leather cases of instruments, resembling the bone-handled razors used for shaving, had in fact been Monsieur Remi's inheritance from his paternal grandfather. It was the opposite of my mother's kitchen, yet as awe-inspiring in its purely masculine way. Oh, but best of all was the chair in which I myself was destined momentarily to sit.

It was the jewel in the king's crown, that chair, and, more than anything else in the room, appeared to have been deliberately constructed for the shape and size of a child, though generally, and despite its small size, its occupants were not children but men in work clothes whose suffering brought even those hulking fellows down to the level of the wailing child. Small, then, but mechanical, with cast-iron foot pedals and levers that suggested a kinship with the mammoth automobiles of the day. It was the only such chair in our entire region and upholstered in leather as soft as the long kid gloves sometimes worn by the young count's wife, and of the same beige color.

But short-lived was the enjoyment I took in these new surroundings. For in the next instant the shutters went crashing open, dawn light filled the room, and there I was, seated in the remarkable chair and wearing an old piece of toweling tied around my neck and hiding my chest. And there was Solange, approaching. She wore a protective apron like that of our local butcher—not at all similar to the apron worn by Maman, which never showed even the faintest bloodstains, as this one did—and was carrying an ivory-handled scaler, the thin blade of which flashed brighter than did any blade swept high in readiness by chef or butcher. I cried aloud, I clutched the armrests of Monsieur Remi's glorious chair, and I clenched my jaws against that sweet concoction composed of equal parts of fear and pain. Around the room grinned the rows of artificial teeth, as Solange's booted foot worked heavily to raise me well into her indifferent grasp. Then with a firm hand she pried open my mouth and—would you believe it?—began randomly stabbing this little tooth or that in an effort to identify which one of all those tiny look-alikes was in fact the foul thing in which the worm burrowed. Here, there, went the tip of the blade, methodically. Time stopped. For me there was nothing but my mouth gripped open, my eyes squeezed shut, and the pain that Solange, if anything, had intensified so as to make it all but unbearable.

Well, it was then that I was attacked from another quarter and awakened to the greatest possible alarm. Oh, but that incredulity, that pure shock, must have served as my anesthesia—which incidentally, and nonmetaphorically, had recently come into Monsieur Remi's possession but was kept under lock and key lest it fall into the hands of his assistant. But incredulity it was that popped my eyes open and stopped my heart, swept away my slightest consciousness of pain. Why? At what? Armand, of course. Solange's blank face and bulging throat, the determination with which she poked and probed, sending my poor teeth toppling one after another, or so it felt, were nothing compared to what I now realized was happening. How could it be? What worse time could Armand have chosen to add his own activity to that of Solange? But it was so. Armand was attempting to come up! To climb from his hiding place! Had I not enough to contend with? Could it be mere curiosity that now fueled the frog into such energetic action? Was he somehow vulnerable to the toothache I thought purely mine? Whatever the reason, whatever had driven Armand awake, suffice it to say that he was fighting his way to the surface, kicking and wriggling like a coal miner worming his way up a tight shaft. So I swallowed, I did my best to fight him down, in the midst of my howling I nonetheless girded myself to force back down the frog as well as the bile, the slime, the nausea with which he was attended. But to no avail. I felt my stomach heave, my windpipe clog, my mouth fill with the swelling shape of that frog, whose burst of determination was obviously as great as that of Solange. Oh, all was lost, I thought, if Solange, whose apron was already freshly soiled, caught so much as a glimpse of Armand's green head protruding over the hapless pillow of my tongue, apparently stuck there in my open mouth and catching his breath.

Then she screamed. She began to shake. Her great white face bore down on mine. And incredulity? Yes, Solange now knew incredulity that exceeded mine by far and in the instant, and for the only time in her life, became a living woman rather than the poor, dull, disinterested creature that it was her fate to be. But in that same instant, her face contorted into a mask of ugliness to match the ugliness that now accosted her astounded eye, she lost control of her scaler and drew back, made a desperate swipe with the merciless tip of the scaler at the edge of my mouth, and screamed again and stared in horror at what lay on the piece of toweling on my chest. Can you imagine the sight? Can you hold your breath forever? Yes, it was Armand's poor tiny severed foot that lay on my chest, as I too saw when I raised up my head and stared in exactly the same disbelief as Solange's. Believe me.

Well, before I knew it, Armand became a fist in my mouth, my throat, and drove himself back down into the turbulent darkness from which he had so foolishly ventured. At the same time Solange dropped the scaler—it sounded like an armload of sabers falling to that old wooden floor—and bravely and with vengeance, like a woman holding a dead rat, snatched the toweling from my chest and crumpled it, her face averted, and disposed of it in a can in one of the corners still dark despite the now risen sun. Then in a stroke she was at me again, this time wielding a pair of iron forceps, and from my little pummeled mouth yanked out not one tooth but two, one of which must have been the carrier of the spiteful worm, just as I was the carrier of my now three-footed frog, for by late afternoon the pain had all but disappeared. However, those two pearly white teeth of mine were never replaced by either living or artificial duplicates, so that to this day there are two gaping spaces to remind me of Solange, who, shortly thereafter, disappeared from our *département,* unable to bear or to divulge my secret, poor woman. What a life must have been hers.

I might add that Solange was the first person but not the last to see Armand, though she was the only person ever to inflict injury on him, except for the occasion of what I, quite wrongly, took to be his death.

Additional "proof," as we have called it, is not necessary? For once we are in accord. And have no fear, I shall not press my advantage and summon up my barrage of "proofs" that a mere frog can cause a war, though so I am inclined to believe.

Which reminds me—my frog's and my father's war, that is—that ours was the first village in that nondescript *département* of ours, perhaps in our entire nation, for all

88

I know, to erect in our village square a memorial to our fallen sons, and this a goodly time before our first son fell. Think of it. Not a soul for kilometers around who did not join the huddled crowd that cold, rainy afternoon for the unveiling. Yes, our luminous flag dropped away at the proper time, and there he stood, a larger-than-life-size replica of all our sons and fathers soon to fall, noble in his ghostly white stone and proud of his uniform, his weapon, and his strangely half-walnut-shaped helmet, which would in fact offer our hero not a jot of protection when the time came. He wore a sharp little beard, though his eyes were sightless. I suppose the beard was intended to indicate that our sons—happily I was not one of them—were already appropriately mature by the time they fell, or would be, despite their youth. The wonderful thing about our monument was that it bore none of the names of those we mustered and sent off to join the shadowy ranks of glory, since of course not one of our villagers had yet fallen, though soon they would, never fear. All seven of them. A mere drop among those whose names were chiseled into our monuments forever, but a gift of sorts nonetheless. How keenly dear Papa wished to have his own name immortalized among them, which was not to be, though that war, great lolling thing of morbid bells and black clouds close to the earth, singled him out more interestingly than he expected. As for me, when the monster finally got under way and I first became aware of cannons and clumsily running men—fodder, as it pleased Papa to call them—I thought that Armand and I could end it all if only they could be persuaded to ram me down into a squat, still-warm cannon barrel and fire us, Armand and me, through the flaming skies to rout whole regiments of the enemy with our awfulness.

For Papa, the beginning of the Great Devastation was a matter of boyish pride. Oh, how he loved his bristling ill-fitting uniform and above all the kepi which sat majestically atop his head and low on his brow. And imagine his delight when he and the young count drove off in the Citroën, Papa at the wheel and in the rear the young count in his tailor-made uniform, and too serious even to wave to his young wife and faithful chef, who were both fluttering thin handkerchiefs at the stately automobile pressed into service, so to speak, as were its newly important occupants.

Poor dear little Maman. She was condemned to grief or worry, one or the other or both, by either son or husband or both. Imagine my mother as young as the young count's wife and prettier, and nothing to justify her existence or to give her the slightest feeling of self-worth except for her skill in practicing the culinary arts for God and the rest of us. Poor dear little Maman, how honorable was her sentimentality. If only she could have seen Armand, just once, and not through the eyes of that pathetic Solange, but through mine.

The first time that Papa returned to us, restraining his proud and boyish smile as he drove the count back into our midst and into the welcoming jubilation of that small crowd of wives and embarrassed peasants—including those several men who had not yet disappeared into the misty rank and file, that is, and also including myself, of course, quite excluded from any pleasure at the poor man's return since his exuberance destroyed the happiness I might have felt at seeing him salute the count and turn to Maman, smiling beyond the limits of decorum and arms wide—on that happy occasion, as I say, Papa kept my mother and me up half the night, listening to his stories and explanations of his good fortune. At least Armand had sense enough to hold his peace while Maman and I indulged in my father's self-infatuation.

Papa did have one minor disappointment, glossed over as swiftly as possible, which was that he had not been assigned to be the count's personal attendant. But there was compensation enough, since our nation's entire army, or at least some lengthy chain of commanding officers responsible for the well-being of all our sons, including Papa, had looked upon him with rare benevolence and good sense.

"Twenty-and-one!" Papa exclaimed more than once throughout that long night. "Twenty-and-one!" Apparently that odd phrase reminded him of my nonexistent grandmother's twenty-two teeth, since he could not refrain from repeating it to himself long after he had conveyed to us its significance. On those three words hung poor Papa's life, or rather his change of life, which was severe indeed.

"More wine, Michel-André?" my sleepy mother would ask, no doubt hoping to hush my father's talking and bring him at last to the verge of sleep.

But *Twenty-and-one,* he would say happily, in total silence to himself and not even mouthing the words, and then launch into another anecdote about the work entrusted to him by the generals. The explanation that for so many hours he managed to withhold from us was simply this: The cavalry! There in a nutshell, as my father put it, was the whole thing.

On what did our great cavalry depend? On what was it founded, as faith was founded on a rock? Horses, of course. And how could our nation's horses be transported to the front, as it was called? By train, of course. And how can horses, hundreds of horses, be hauled about by train? In boxcars! What else? exclaimed Papa with a snap of his fingers. But could our precious horses travel alone? Indeed they could not. Horses must be tended by men! How else could they eat or drink, gathered together in near darkness on their long journeys to the fields of mud and valor that awaited them, except thanks to the industry of men? And how could these horses, sensitive creatures that they were, be calmed, and hence saved from panic and resultant injury as they approached the random cannonade of battle and the dreadful fright that must attend it? By the care and reassurance of men, of course. Exactly. Well, we must understand, said Papa, speaking like the schoolmaster in uniform that he always wished to be, whether he knew it or not, that our boxcars were by no means large. They were small, in fact. And rickety. But mainly small. Precision was needed. Here it was that our military minds came forth and saved the day. They measured the capacity of the boxcar. Think of it! No wonder such men command the respect they do. Well, it was an established fact, then, that a single boxcar could hold twenty horses, no more, no fewer, and in addition one man, exactly one man, to minister to the needs, physical and temperamental, of the twenty horses who had fallen to his responsibility. And it was a grave responsibility, said my Papa, even down to ridding the boxcars of manure when circumstances permitted.

So it was that *Twenty-and-one* was scrawled in chalk on every boxcar containing a precious cargo of living horses and industrious, quick-witted man. *Twenty horses and one man.* Why, it could not be plainer! And if these boxcars specially loaded were not so marked, where might our precious horses find themselves? What, for instance, could our field kitchens do with horses? Or artillery units in need of shells? Or imagine field hospitals suddenly deluged not with crates of morphine but with horses! Disaster, Marie, as Papa said, smiling and tossing off his glass as the late hour cloaked Maman and me in some unbearable dream.

Finally, said Papa, it was to the everlasting credit of the general who came across Papa's name, on whichever lengthy list it was inscribed upon, to recognize him as a man of the earth and so to order him forthwith to serve in the cavalry, not as a rider, of course—Papa had never been on a horse in his life, as his record must have clearly stated—but as one of those men capable of the almost impossible duty of accompanying boxcar after boxcar of horses to the front, which by now had become one of Papa's favorite words.

"How marvelous, Michel-André," whispered my mother, "but it is time for bed. After all, tomorrow you must return to duty."

No doubt most young children find themselves wondrously alerted to anything having to do with horses. But not I. That night I shared Maman's lack of interest in all that dear Papa had said, and found nothing glorious in my father's return to us as a soldier, or in the boxcars that to him, but not to me, were nothing less than flaming chariots. A groom in the cavalry, that's where my Papa had landed. Even that night he smelled faintly of oats in a bucket and the rank manure that it had been his recent lot to shovel. At least, as were his closing words that night, members of the cavalry were likely to live to sport their medals, as most of those poor devils in the infantry, which were his words, were not. But even this fact dulled and tarnished the father I should have admired that night yet could not. A groom, that's what he was, and had not even attained the rank of corporal! Poor man.

However, there was much to excite me and to engage my interest in Papa's second return to us, which, incidentally, was his last. In the first place, he came back to us not at the wheel of the count's beige-colored limousine but in the rear of a small battered military truck. It was not Papa who held the auto door for the count but instead the driver of the truck who, cigarette dangling from the corner of his mouth, helped my father climb to the ground. He was haggard. He was not smiling. Those who met him—the count's wife, little Christophe's mother, a few peasant women, and Maman, of course—were a forlorn group huddled bareheaded in a light snow and attempting to hide their grief. All but myself, that is. I was not grieving! Quite the opposite! For the man who stood before us, leaning in angry embarrassment on two wooden crutches, was not the braggart who had left us a mere few months earlier. Not at all. Oh, he was missing a leg! The right leg! And that was the marvel that sent my spirits soaring! After all, I had never seen a man with only one leg, and my father's missing leg, the leg that none of us would ever see again, so engaged my fancy that even Armand began to convey his envy, despite his own missing paw or foot, or hand as I still prefer to think of it. So what did I do, shocking those grieving women to the core? Why, suddenly unable to bear any further my pain and pleasure—the first firing up my belly anew, thanks to Armand, the second possessing my entire being, thanks to Papa—I tore my own hand free from Maman's and rushed forward and embraced Papa's remaining leg. I confess that it was nearly as enticing as its missing partner, and I hugged it with an affection that was entirely new to me and certainly to my father.

"Welcome home, Papa!" I cried, much to my poor mother's consternation and my father's indifference. How I hugged his unfeeling, remaining leg while darting secret looks at the trouser leg pinned up on the stump of the other. Did I care that he smelled like a groom? Did I care that on his chest he wore no small ribbons indicative of this medal or that yet to come? Not at all! He was wounded! He was a marvel! Was that not what I had wished of him from the start? It was! It was!

Well, it was just like poor Papa to take no notice of me and to remain indifferent to the sentiments—though unusual, we must admit—which I had just displayed. Yes, indifferent, very like the dead man dragged about the streets of our capital by an old woman dressed in white. Why, he did not even acknowledge what we all heard my mother say. He was too angry to care that her happiness lay in the fact that he was still alive, though there in the snow his missing leg had already begun to drag her down just as it tossed me, even in that gloomy scene, high in the air.

My father rarely talked to either wife or son after his second return. Just once, while sitting hunched over in his cold corner, hated crutches propped at his side, did he make clear to Maman and me what had happened. There was a shell burst, a direct hit, to use the language of those familiar with such things, which at the time infuriated my father as much as if that shell burst had destroyed the field hospital, morphine included, to which he had in fact been carried. It was an act of indecency to fire artillery pieces at innocent horses! An act of bestiality comparable to firing upon those supposedly protected by the large red cross painted on the top of the sagging tent. But there it was. An explosion. A boxcar filled with the sounds of squealing and kicking, even as that boxcar flew apart into the wintry air. And the heads. The severed heads of the frantic horses, in the midst of which lay his own leg, never again to be discovered or even recognized as such. And what was one man's leg compared with even one head in that bloody heap? Nothing. Nothing at all. Why, each dead horse's head appeared to my father to be crying aloud for help as strongly as might any man in the first moments of amputation. Relief! Relief! He heard them crying together.

Well, this story, soon to be buried alive, so to speak, in my father's lifelong anger, left my poor mother weeping, I can tell you, and myself with a thoroughly newfound interest in horses—though only in maimed horses, I confess. And may I confess that I took pleasure in my father's inability to find in himself the ordinary cripple's good humor shared inevitably with a blind man? So it was. My father was not the sort of man to tolerate a frog in his stomach. And it was this fact that was his undoing. But what actually had happened? Why, in losing his leg and the few horses in his charge, he had lost his boyish good humor. And at precisely the time when I lost my own boyhood in exchange for manhood, or at least for as much manhood as I wanted. To whom? Why, to Christophe's mother, of course. Yes, it was thanks to that unwashed, unkempt woman, who was the same age as my own mother and the count's wife, or perhaps I should say widow—coincidence is the hallmark of the creative mind—that I saw what I wanted to see, smelled what I wanted to smell, touched what I wanted to touch. Yes, in all her final deprivation she proved to be a generous soul, that wicked woman, who might well have taught the young count's wife a trick or two. What a glistening gift was her gift to me! And as anyone might readily understand, it preserved my innocence while shattering my boyhood as totally as that whistling shell had shattered my father's boxcar. Well, it takes a poisoner to introduce the poisoned mind to manhood.

Of the two of us, it was my father who was the first to exchange life at the Domaine Ardente for that other life at Saint-Mamès. The day he left Maman and me, she, poor creature, reassured me that he would be happier by far at Saint-Mamès, not knowing, of course, how delighted I was to see him go, though at the time I had not the slightest idea how swiftly I would follow in his one-legged footsteps. My secret, you see, finally became too much even for my long-suffering Maman. Yes, frog or no frog, war or no war, and widow and poisoner notwithstanding, poor dear Papa and I were not yet done with each other, as we shall see.

The count? Well, that brave, kind, illustrious man did not come home to us. In fact his was the first name to be chiseled onto our village monument, which was exactly as he would have wanted it, since clearly it was the obligation of our shattered aristocracy to lead the way for our shattered populace.

Anatole, Comte de Beauval, August 1882–January 1915
Oh, dear sweet Maman! I cannot live without you!

CHAPTER TWO
Saint-Mamès

IT HAS ALWAYS BEEN my firm belief that it was the young count's widow who arranged for my relocation, so to speak, from the Domaine Ardente to Saint-Mamès. No doubt that young woman had reason enough to revenge herself on young Pascal, as I was called by then, especially in those prime years when her widowhood forbade her womanhood. There was no comparison between the innocence of the child who appeared one day on the very threshold of her boudoir and the bodily evidence of the boy whose masculinity, no matter the various shapes it took or because of them, was already a legend on that estate deprived, as were so many, of its significant men. How they must have talked, those few old illiterates whose age and wits had saved them from the great slaughtering, mouthing their yellow cigarettes and slapping their thighs whenever they gleaned that I had once more entrusted myself to little Christophe's mother, who herself spread the rumor of my prowess, the more remarkable for its unconventionality. Yes, little Christophe's mother was pleased enough to have me, and yes, the young count's wife must indeed have been envious and, knowing as she did about Armand from my poor mother, must certainly have arranged in secret for my removal from the Domaine Ardente, for my own good as she must have told herself and my Maman, not believing a word of it.

Yet what wonderful irony that what she said but did not believe proved that she was in fact correct, a situation of which she never knew. That is, from the beginning I had simply accepted as given that any stage set provided for this or that period of my life would in fact be appropriate to my well-being and conducive to the fullest possible expression of the life that was then mine. Thus the Domaine Ardente could not have contributed more perfectly to my good childhood, nor Saint-Mamès to my early stages of manhood, nor Madame Fromage's brothel to my gathering interests as a young man. An aristocratic estate, an asylum, the world of whoredom, in which for a time I served as both concierge and darling of Madame Fromage herself and those other females who found me as compliant and amazing as I did them. Well, there we have it, the stage sets I did not seek but welcomed, the ironic congruence between where I was and what I was.

Apprehensive about Saint-Mamès? Not at all. Whether or not such places as Saint-Mamès were intended to protect those like myself from nonbelievers, or to protect nonbelievers from those like myself, has little relevance to me, to Armand, or to those qualities of mind we share. The more I grew, the more I throve on the ironies for which I was not responsible, one of which was that but to enter

Saint-Mamès was to be accepted for what you were. Thus from the outset I was known there as the boy who harbored a frog in his stomach, with no more surprise or curiosity than if I had gone about holding my severed head under my arm. And the ultimate irony about Saint-Mamès is that that particular saint—Saint-Mamès—is the patron saint of the stomach. From those afflicted with the slightest twinge of pain in the lower abdomen to those bent double as a matter of course, or unable to eat or to rid themselves of what they had unwisely eaten, all such victims of the stomach flocked to worship Saint-Mamès and beg relief, exactly as the other sick armies crawled to their various shrines in the hopes of leaving behind their crutches.

Miss Maman? Of course I missed Maman—from the start—and wondered why she did not visit me, which she never did, or why she did not send me a few loving, encouraging words on paper. But on that score there was only mysterious silence. Perhaps she thought that at last I was old enough to live without her, an impossibility that makes me grieve even now, or perhaps, once rid of both Papa and me, she could not bear the emptiness that so much as a thought of us would deepen. But I longed to see Maman entering Saint-Mamès in search of me, smiling and carrying on her arm a wicker basket filled with preserves which she herself had prepared from the glorious fruit of the Domaine Ardente. Yet there was never a sight of her, never the sound of her voice. I lay awake weeping for Maman and wishing that the pain inflicted on me by

Armand would dissolve once and for all my memories of Maman and leave me with nothing, which of course it did not, and this at a time when I was twelve or fourteen years of age, with both feet squarely planted over the threshold of young manhood.

It has always given me special delight that by and large I have found myself provided with someone to remind me of my Maman, if not replace her, and some counterpart to Papa. In Saint-Mamès this parental repetition took the form of Dr. Chapôte, who in appearance should have been director of a bank instead of an asylum, and the woman who at least in name was his wife. Madame Chapôte. Marie-Claude. It was rumored that she herself had once been a patient in Saint-Mamès, before the arrival of Dr. Chapôte, that is, who found her one day tearing her hair and laughing, and ended that kind of behavior by marrying her. I would have put no credence in such a rumor except for the fact that for all the years she lived among us as the doctor's wife, and until her disappearance—for she did in fact disappear, with the huskiest and cruelest of our male nurses—her greatest pleasure was in riding her ancient black bicycle, long skirts flying, bell ringing, and laughing and waving at each and every one of us she passed, hailing us with her pealing good spirits and showing, to the quick eye and with her feet off the pedals and her extended legs spread wide, what her long skirts ordinarily concealed. Surely Madame Chapôte on her bicycle might well have been a vestige of her former identity as inmate.

Credibility, as we now know, gets not the slightest nod from me, even in passing. In fact, the less credible the events of my life, the better, which brings me all at once to Papa. Neither one of us was aware of the other's presence in this famous, overpopulated asylum, while both of us had already spent long years in the place, he nursing the latent violence of his self-pity, I enjoying the renown of Armand. But one day, against all odds, shortly before the hour of noon, in a curiously vacated and graveled space between two buildings with barred windows, there he was, there I was, Papa with his crutches, I not so different from the Tadpole I had always been, additional years and pounds and height notwithstanding. He stopped. He cast a disfigured shadow. He showed no surprise at seeing me. And then, and as if time and our infirmities had had not the slightest effect on us, he stared at me, licked his lips, and spoke.

"She's gone."

Had I heard aright?

He stooped and towered above me. His thick hair was still parted in the middle but had turned a yellowish iron gray, and he still wore the uniform he had refused to give up when he had first come back to us. Worst of all, his long face was more contorted than ever in the fury of self-pity. There he was, Papa, staring down at me with his brows knit and the hands with which he helped to brace himself on his crutches grown large and shapeless thanks to his dead weight. Ruined Papa. Out of the blue.

But what did he mean? What had he meant?

"She's gone," he repeated, in tones of accusation that were leveled at me alone. And then those two words struck home.

Maman! I cried to myself, still looking up at him with my wide, thin lips parted and my hair bristling, a young man of fourteen—twelve, then! whatever you will!—my face suffused in the innocence that the presence of Papa always induced in me, to protect me no doubt from what I really felt toward him. Maman, of course. And in the sentimental, euphemistic language he always used, "gone" meant one thing only. Dead. But how could she in fact be dead? How could she have died? She was younger by more than years than my Papa, she was the heroine of "The Cook's Prayer." How then could it be so? But it was.

Whereupon, and still looking up at Papa, I felt my facial expression beginning to change. I felt it stretch, I felt my mouth assume the shape of an immense oval, and I stooped slightly, as if I had been kicked in the stomach by a horse—the pain was that great—while for the second time in my life Armand was making his ascent. Yes, arising from the depths of me to expose himself like a monster under the command of some black magician and do my bidding, though as yet I had not even formulated the idea of what I wished him to do.

My torso was bent forward in pain, my head was bent backward and up so that I might face Papa at last. I cupped my hands so as to make of them a little bowl or dish beneath my mouth. All was silence; not one face peered down at us from between rusty bars. And then, *Blurp! Blurp!* And with this sound, deeper and more resonant than any basso sound in a plugged-up drain in an abandoned church, Armand waited, surveying the tall old cripple from my open mouth, and then popped out and settled himself compactly in my waiting hands. As simple as that.

Nothing more. Except that Papa went white, his eyes started from his head, and his crutches broke! Yes, in several crucial places his wooden crutches, so long in use by now, simply splintered and broke into pieces and collapsed from beneath his hands and shoulders while Armand and I looked on.

Down he crashed, eyes still bursting with disbelief, a thread of redness trickling from one nostril, his initial pallor turned the color of dead clay. With both hands I stuffed Armand back into my mouth—perfectly aware in passing that once freed he was reluctant to return to the dark confines of his living cave. Papa was staring up at me. Crumpled as he was on the gravel, he looked like an enormous beast of burden succumbing at last to loads too heavy to pull. Then—what new shock was this?—then once more he spoke.

"Poor Pascal."

Papa, in the death throes induced by my own Armand, nonetheless devoting his last words to me? But why? For having to live with the knowledge that Maman was dead? Or could he possibly have pitied me for having to live alone in this world without the help and guidance of my own Papa? Could he in the end have hit upon such an egoistic thought? How like Papa of old, I thought—always sentimental, always misguided. At least my frog, in striking him down, had rid him of the anger in which everyone else had thought he would surely die. Better that he think of me, no matter how unjustifiably, than of himself in this final moment.

I rose to my feet. The stunning evidence of Armand's power, greater than I had ever dreamt, spoke for itself. Armand was the killer, but it was I who had called him forth. Why, given what had happened, I might as well have beaten Papa to death with a club. Sometimes I regret that I did not. On the other hand, the killing caused by my frog of course sufficed. What an elegant barbarity! What an amazing capability! I still feel his smelly, slippery body cupped in my palms that day, still see Papa's response. And did I not hear a vast approaching sound like that of the distant nighttime frogs of my childhood? I did, except that what I heard were cheers, wave after wave of cheers coming from this direction and that, from invisible fields and from stone buildings far out of sight. Yes, all of Saint-Mamès was softly cheering, and my pain was gone.

The crutches? Those miserable crutches? Yes, he simply dropped them, that's all. Are you satisfied? But you will not make me give up the cheering. It still rings in my head.

Au revoir, Papa.

The immediate aftermath of my father's death was to me as unpredictable as had been the death itself, no matter

how the prospect of it had been ingrained in me before-
hand, and in Armand. For without thinking, I turned
away from Papa's remains and set off possessed of but a
single objective. It was not Papa that concerned me or the
fact that he existed no more, but Maman. And I knew
what I must find, at once, without delay of any sort. So
for the first time in the half-dozen years or perhaps the
decade that I had lived in Saint-Mamès, I left my asylum
and, as fast as I could, walked the empty road bordered
by plane trees to the village whose church spire I could
see in the distance. I reached the dreary little gardens sur-
rounding the village, walked directly to the unfamiliar
church—for it was a church I sought—and entered its
cool darkness and smells of wax and dust and fresh flowers
on the altar. There was much to engage my sensual interests if I had bothered to seek out the church objectively,
for pleasure only—the hardness of stone, the peeling gold
on the various sculpted figures inhabiting the different
parts of this place, the few candles still dripping and flick-
ering on the ingenious spikes that held them upright in
the drafts of dead air that made my skin prickle—but my
purpose had nothing to do with pleasure in any familiar
sense. And certainly not with solace. Once inside, alone
inside, did I make my way to the altar? Or move about
in selfish exploration? I did not. But rather, and without
a moment's hesitation, I made my way to the rear of the
church, where I found what I wanted, despite my ignorance of all things pertaining to the church, such as wed-
dings, funerals, baptism. Yet there it was, propped against

a wall in shadows and cobwebs, a device that looked like a stretcher of sorts or a ladder for climbing to inedible apples but was in fact intended to bear the weight of coffins. How did I know that this curious piece of equipment existed? Ready with its four extending wooden handles polished by the sweaty palms of all that procession of grieving men who had employed it to transport at a snail's pace the burdens for which they had grieved? I have no idea. After all, I am not able to answer every question that comes to mind. Speculations aside, I went directly to what I sought but had never seen and stood before it as in a crypt, admiring the simplicity of the thing where it stood propped against the wall and conceiving to myself the silent passages, the bodies that had been carried from this little church to the chalky walled-in garden, so to speak, of the dead. And Maman? Had she too been carried on a black lacquered litter, indistinguishable from the one before which I stood? Exactly. I had no interest in tombs or graves or in the talismans of death, or in the congregation of which I alone should have been a member, but was interested only in the sight of this simple frame, whose function had been to carry away once and for all my own Maman.

After a few such minutes, seeing in my mind's eye the litter standing horizontally on its stubby legs on the uneven stone slabs that composed the floor, burdened with its final burden, the only one I cared about, I turned on my heel and made my way from the church, indifferent to the booming sound of my footsteps or to the unseemly sound of the door that crashed shut behind me. But do you know, once born in me, this compulsion never faded, so that as often as the mood has come upon me I have visited one such house of worship or another, as I have described. If this makes me a churchgoer, then so be it. It was thanks to this first such excursion of mine that I met Marthe, and that I was quite stunned with happiness at the coincidence—yes, another and another—that near Madame Fromage's hotel, as it once was, there stood the shabbiest little church I could have wished for, but the very one that had produced a vision worthy of a cathedral, as we shall see.

Cause and effect? How like you to produce that old saw out of your bag of tricks! If you had been listening you would already know how much I deplore those efforts to organize ourselves safely, according to some sensible proposition. I despise the philosopher as much as I do the priest, though the church is at least serious, vaguely belonging as it does in the same category with Saint-Mamès. My own beliefs? Well, hear me out. I believe in Maman. In Armand. In myself. All the rest is rubbish, except perhaps for Saint-Mamès, where, as I have made plain, I still languish.

Have I indicated the extent of this ever changing place, have I established it as the great architectural conglomerate it is, thanks to its varying uses down the epochs? Bars? Yes, some of our more nondescript buildings guard those within with fine fat bars that leave the clinging hand red with rust and the sensation of hexagonal iron that fills the palm. But châteaux? Yes, we have several, one through which we are admitted into Saint-Mamès and two, I believe, that are still decaying into the sumptuous derelicts that they are—splendid nests for spiders, I might add. On top of all this, and as final evidence of man's changing intents and labors down the epochs I just mentioned, there are the remains of the convent where the nuns that came and went across the sands of Saint-Mamès, and were perhaps its first settlers, devoted their energies to that brief colony of exiled wretches suffering from *Bacillus leprae*—worse luck they!—though these remains of the former leper house are generally empty, consisting of little more than a ruined chapel, a roofless dormitory, and a weed-drenched cloister, rarely inhabited or visited, except by crows. And of course we have several working farms and all the outbuildings associated therewith, and a well-preserved old barn housing the stone tubs in which some of us are brought round to our senses by cold water and even ice. Church? No, there is not a church anywhere to be found in Saint-Mamès, at least as far as my own explorations, incomplete as they are, admittedly, have uncovered. If we had had a church at Saint-Mamès, of course I would not have walked to the nearby village church and so would have failed to meet Marthe, devoted little girl that she proved to be.

But more? Anything else? Yes indeed, for a mere stone's throw from our admitting building—the château in which there lives no count or seductive countess, the worse for me—stands a small latter-day manor house in excellent repair, a dwelling most anomalous, since amidst all the other structures of Saint-Mamès it alone suggests normalcy and family life. And what is this place with its pretty porticoes and geometric gardens in full bloom? Home of our medical director and chief administrator, of course, and his wife. Madame Chapôte. Marie-Claude. As attested by the gleaming brass plaque beside the door. Children? No children, *mon dieu!* How could I have been so very favored by Marie-Claude if there had been tiny ones forever scampering between us and insidiously hiding in Madame's boudoir when our director was traveling, which he often did? And then there would have been the further inconvenience of the nursemaid. But all this, as I say, she and I were spared.

Well, there we have our aerial view of Saint-Mamès, as seen perhaps by Armand in the claws of that singing crow—Heaven forbid!—and except for the fields and stands of trees and brooks and streams and, threading the entirety, the dirt roads and sand or pebbled paths that begin at some doorway and strike off purposefully and then stop, as if the proud planner had lost heart. But here, and exactly in the fashion of one of the most touted of those national treasures of ours, one of our hypocritical, socially oriented writers of tomes that document, while purporting to be works of the imagination, only our city life and family life, consisting for the most part of rancor and *haute cuisine*—here, as I say, I may as well complete my essential cast of characters who first surrounded me in Saint-Mamès. I have already alluded to Bocage but not named him, as I do now, mainly to add that this massive man, sadist if ever there was one—how advanced is my terminology!—took a special liking to me even before it was common knowledge that I was the favorite of the director's wife, and never caused me a moment's pain. Then there was Bocage's confrere Lulu, another hulking figure but with worried eyes, who, like Bocage, could subdue even the most terrifying of our vast band. These two, Bocage and Lulu, lowliest in the hierarchy of Saint-Mamès's inhabitants, detained or otherwise, are the last worth naming, which I do only because of my inability to forgive Bocage and because, when the occasion arose, it was Lulu who restrained me, as the situation required, and with remarkable gentleness to say the least.

Tomes? Oh, there are many tomes in Dr. Chapôte's private study, and I must tell you, I despise the lot of them as well as the very idea of tome. To what fatuousness does its size attest! To what smug labors and running off at the mouth! To what blowing of one's own horn does it lead! and straight down the road to becoming a national treasure! Well, that road is not for me. I detest the road to honor, lined as it is with thousands of misty-eyed citizens who cannot trust their senses even when our great author stops to relieve himself and eat a five-hour meal. But how do I have any knowledge of tomes and Dr. Chapôte's private study with its dark red walls and bookcases to the ceiling and polished desk large enough to sleep on? Because I am seated at that very desk! Yes, it is here at the desk at which the poor man used to prepare his medical tracts that I prepare my miniature tome. Exactly.

There is no question but that I owe my privileged place in Saint-Mamès and at its director's desk to Madame Chapôte herself, as I have suggested. But I was groomed for this position of mine in our institution and in Marie-Claude's affections only by the gradual revelation of my cooking abilities and, more important, by little Marthe, the child who had followed me that day from the village church back to Saint-Mamès and through the void of its main gate.

It took me half the distance down that empty road between church and asylum to detect her presence, preoccupied as I was by what I had seen in the consecrated darkness only moments before. But detect it I did, hearing diminutive footsteps slow with mine, stop with mine, proceed once more in perfect tune with mine. Finally I stopped and turned to face my benign pursuer, whereupon she, so small, so thin, so pathetic in her long gray old-woman's dress, feigned ignorance, scanning the bleak fields visible between the plane trees on either side of us, and then the empty heavens. I stood my ground, hands on hips, scowling. She faced me, dared to come a few paces closer, stopped, looked away. And so forth. Each time stopping, acting the part of the innocent and then, considering it safe to do so, approaching still closer, her white face as empty of expression as the countryside, the disappearing village, the walls of Saint-Mamès now outlined on the horizon—and never before had I been so aware of the sheer mystery of attraction as I was then. Marthe approached in her strange rhythm of fits and starts, gauging her distance and my reaction to its diminishment, until she was within an arm's length of me. Then I turned once more toward Saint-Mamès.

But did that local saint exist? In flesh and blood? Or was Saint-Mamès only the ecclesiastical figment after which our thriving asylum took its name? In flesh and blood, if you will. Or at least in wood, which I might easily argue is one and the same. I have seen him. I have lain at his feet. I have studied his sad eyes even while succumbing to the pain of which he is empowered to relieve us. And marvel of all marvels, it was thanks to my young guide, Marthe, that I first came upon our famous saint, so cleverly hidden that she and I might have been the only ones to have found him out. Guide? Yes, guide indeed, for by the time Marthe and I had actually set foot within the realm of darkness and nonconformity, Marthe was no longer following along behind me but had taken the lead.

I am not a sentimentalist, as must be evident by now. Anything but that. On the other hand, I am not a monster. Hardly. I have not the slightest wish to deny the tenderness that Marthe inspired in me between church and hiding place of Saint-Mamès, and over a period of time too long to confine by measurement. Tenderness, then, to which I still admit, despite her besting of me, so to speak, and the unexpectedness of her deceit, which of course I forgave the very moment it first emerged.

On the other hand, I confess I felt a certain superiority to my young guide and her overtrustful nature, as I so wrongly thought of it, even as she led me between this pair of massive old buildings or that, disregarding the occasional waving hand or shouts of greeting, and out through the thinning crowds and growing emptiness until our path disappeared and we were surrounded by weeds and brambles. Here my skepticism as to what she was about increased, as did my irritation at the thickets and sharp entanglements of natural growth that impeded our progress. Her clothing was snagged; we could not avoid the thorns. From away in the distance I heard the ringing of Madame Chapôte sailing along on her bicycle, and paused to lick a sudden scratch on the back of my hand.

Then, and just in time, we arrived. For there in a small clearing only mildly overgrown and shaded by large intrusive oaks stood the abandoned stones and partial walls of what I immediately recognized as the convent in which the nuns of old gave asylum to lepers as clearly belled as Madame Chapôte's bicycle.

We walked several times around the cloister, stumbling on bits of rubble and passing through shafts of sunlight that came down upon us from the various openings in the cloister roof. By now Marthe had adjusted her pace and position so as to be walking all but at my side, and I was aware beyond a doubt of her closeness. After all,

Marthe's purpose displayed itself, finally, in an erotic intelligence unmatched by that of any adult woman I have known before or since. She was not mute, though she gave that impression. She was not an albino, but nearly so. How could anyone resist such translucent skin and pale hair?

Well, her enticement was nothing other than to the convent chapel, or what was left of it, and the statue of Saint-Mamès himself. To this day I have no idea how she knew what irresistible chords she would strike by confronting me with that wooden image of the saint atop his pedestal and unsheltered from passing storms and hovering masses of small birds. My protector in the sepulchral darkness filled with light.

Anyone would have assumed that this, the last likeness of Saint-Mamès, would have been the size of a living man and adorned with the usual golden trappings associated with the holiness of saints. Not so. Not for him any richness of apparel or loftiness of size or expression. He was small, standing perhaps a meter tall, and, in his long brown shabby cloak, resembled the shepherd in the midst of his flock. It was not the sadness of humility that I saw in his eyes, though that too, but the sadness of someone long the stoic victim of unendurable pain. I recognized it at once, as the tiny birds fluttered around him and Marthe drew ever closer to my thick person, since after all I was convinced that my own eyes occasionally drooped with the exact same forbearance as the saint's. And yet—and this is not a contradiction—that small wooden figure loomed as large to me as any man, perhaps larger. If it is possible for a skeptic to be enthralled, then I was enthralled.

Meanwhile, Marthe had edged herself not only closer to my person but into a position facing me. In the mere instant that I looked up at Saint-Mamès—remember that he stood much taller than I did thanks to his pedestal— Marthe took advantage of my distraction and came between myself and the saint. The birds, like sacred bees or lively bats whose skeletal composition was not so very different from Armand's, swarmed most unnaturally about the wooden figure whose pained eyes had looked down sightlessly on nun and leper, until the last of them had disappeared forever, and then on nothing at all. The mingling smell of dust and leaves surrounded us. The warm light felt as if it would never change. The harder I looked up at Saint-Mamès, the more I became aware of Marthe's small face, white with intensity. But what was it that Saint-Mamès held cupped in his gentle hands, locked together at the base of his torso? What strange sack? What shape that no peasant ever bore on his shoulders? His stomach, of course! His own stomach! Even as I recognized that irregular bloated thing, which could only have been anatomical in nature, I felt something as faint as a breath against my own stomach and heard muffled sounds pressing into me.

Marthe, of course, Marthe was humming as softly as possible into the stomach that I could not hold in my hands but was mine. Yes, humming. But why? What did she mean to do? What tentative exploration was she undertaking with one of her small hands? Well, she was humming to Armand, as suddenly I understood, and groping in my clothes instinctively so as to make me even more helplessly pliant, though pleasurably so, than did the sadness in the eyes of Saint-Mamès or the burden he carried in his swathed and gently curving arms and cupped hands.

Irresistible tactics, and from a girl so young! Hypnotic, as she must have known this episode would prove to both Armand and me. *Voilà!* It did not take long for that frog of mine to show himself, for the second time on this remarkable day, and not a moment too soon to save me from the increasing determination of Marthe's childish fingers.

Flesh, you say? So you remember my promise! But this is not the moment for its fulfillment. Not here. I have no intention of exposing the flesh of a small girl whom I did not once see stripped of her clothing. Whatever transpired between Marthe and myself, the glorious light of indecency, or its opposite, never in any way brought to our minds so much as a single thought of nudity, hers or mine.

At any rate I was overwhelmed—beside myself or indeed frantic, if you will—to return the steadfast blueness in the eyes of Saint-Mamès and, all at once, to understand that the stomach he carried was not empty. Even as I, like Armand, succumbed to Marthe's musical breath, and marveled at her ingenuity, and found myself plagued by the why or how of it all, I understood Marthe's plan. For as I have already suggested, Armand was what she sought, and not myself. Again as I have already suggested, Armand gave himself to Marthe's plan and the musical sound of her humming—childish, womanly—with what I can only describe as oily slickness, his rise to meet her appeal being that swift, that smooth. One moment he was dormant, the next he was in my mouth and demanding to be seen by the little girl who of course reminded him of Vivonne. No elbowing, then, no angular kicking and pushing as he fought his way up to the light of day, no sensation of scratchy bones to make me choke, or of bloatedness filling my oral cavity so that I wanted only to eject him for once and all from my mouth. Not at all. For quick as a flash he had risen, with the least possible discomfort to me, while I merely opened my mouth as a matter of course and happily allowed Armand to sit blinking on his door-step, so to speak.

The humming stopped, the rhythm of Marthe's fingers slowed to a standstill, in the light that flickered thanks to the action of the fluttering birds, suddenly Marthe's face was no longer pressed against me but turned up to what she could see of the frog so obviously at rest in my open mouth. She did not smile—I never saw Marthe smile—but her shallow translucent face reflected in every small perfect feature the extent of her curiosity joined at last to the sight of the little creature that had so engrossed her in the first place.

By now I had forgotten Saint-Mamès entirely and was aware only of Marthe, standing on her toes and offering up her sad yet dazzling little face not to me but to Ar-

121

mand. Whereupon this train of perception, or something
like it, forced upon me the full nature of Marthe's yearning for Armand, and not only of how much she wanted
to see him but of how strongly she wanted to take him
from me. Even if Marthe had no intention of going quite
that far, still, as it suddenly occurred to me, the presence
of that small girl concentrating as she was on Armand
might well be enough to cause my frog suddenly to jump.
What then? Obviously, were Armand to leap from my
mouth with all his regained youth in bloom—his injury
sustained in my childhood notwithstanding—he might of
course land happily at Marthe's feet, and then—then?—
with another and more unexpected leap, be gone. The
rubble, the innumerable hiding places in which he might
conceal himself, the grasses intruding into this spare and
ceremonial place—this very spot in which we stood was
too chaotic to risk so much as cupping Armand in my
hands and lowering him to the child's gaze. Why, surely
it would take nothing more than a single lapse in my
attention, and my hands might relax, and away might leap
Armand, as swiftly as he might have leapt from my aston-
ished mouth.

No such dreadful thing occurred. Though I had no
reason to suspect Armand of having any inclination toward a freedom other than what he had long ago chosen
for himself within that part of me cradled by Saint-Mamès
in his wooden arms, or to suspect Armand of abandoning
his loving Vivonne the moment she came to life in this
fashion, nonetheless I was seized with panic at the unal-

terable damage that Marthe might do, and prevented it. No matter the disappointment that showed on her generally expressionless little face—a face worthy of the religious artist's more spectacular creations—I closed my mouth and felt a reluctant Armand submit himself to my will. It was the first time that I knew the panic of losing the very frog who caused me such pain yet who was also the miraculous extension of my pride and power. I was to experience this same panic once more, and in a form so extreme as to cause within a breath the bursting of my very self. Once, in time to come, I was very nearly to lose Armand forever. That second bout of panic was, I must say, enough. From that moment forward I safeguarded Armand for the treasure he still remains.

That day, then, Marthe saw no more of my frog.

Her absences were long and many. Yet each time she sought me out, unannounced, unexpected, I had no choice but to join her in silent greeting. I knew as well as she did what we were about, or what she sought of me and why I was so helplessly cooperative. She did not always seize my hand, she did not always engage in her childishly inspired act of humming to the suddenly attentive Armand, she did not always remember to work her fingers into my clothing. Yet the result was inevitably the same. One way or another we always found a sandy space so open, or an empty walled-in area of old stone so smooth, that there was little or no risk of losing Armand, even had he attempted, in a single leap, to vanish. In safe vastness I called him forth and held him to the level of Marthe's little eyes, intense with joy. It went so far that I allowed Armand to sit between us on the warm stones of some abandoned threshing floor, where we knelt and studied my frog like children comparing for the first time their specific anatomical differences.

Despite all that I had put him through, despite all the stretching and pulling that I, for instance, had suffered in growth, Armand had not changed, as there before our eyes he demonstrated. Of course he was never exactly the same, on one occasion bloated to twice the size of my fist and brownish in color, and on another once more the blue and greenish colors that had flashed or dripped from his body when he had first appeared to me. On some days, as Marthe and I lowered our heads together, she absorbing all she saw in the squatting frog, I shifting my attention back and forth from frog to girl, he acquired all the glistening substance of a handful of wet clay. Thus we watched him, and all the while he was breathing and blinking the large dark eyes that once, in my childhood, had cowed me with accusation or magic. There were even days when, again in some open space and under a watchful sky, I not only set him down, as Marthe wished me to, but went much farther and entrusted him to Marthe's own hands. Oh, indeed I felt a few spasms of anxiety as I did so and saw my frog cupped in what I can only call her angelic palms and fingers, and saw as well the slight parting and rounding of Marthe's lips. Naturally I had no actual need for concern, since Marthe never betrayed me and always handed back my almighty frog when I requested that she do so, though on such occasions I noticed her reluctance, which was the difficulty she had in hearing my voice, understanding my wishes, giving up her visual and tactile immersion in the frog that was, after all, mine.

Sometimes I thought that Marthe must have carried away with her the taste of my frog, though she gave me no reason for such a poetic inclination. Marthe obeyed me. And if she had not? And I had lost Armand not to some putrid cistern of old but to that child's sweet darkness? Who knows what such a happenstance might have called forth from my unpredictable nature?

Once, but only once, I held cupped in my palms as lightly but firmly as I might have held an empty but unbroken egg the small oval face of Marthe, who cast up at me a steady look of appeal such as I never saw in the eyes of Armand. And once, but only once, I leaned down and smelled the breath that came only from Marthe's mouth and could only have been her own.

The last I saw of her was on a cold wintry day when Marthe, dressed in her poor family's heirloom bridal gown, which with veil and train and thickness of its yellowed satin buried what was left of the child I had once known, gave herself away in marriage, exactly as had Marie-Claude and my own dear Maman before her. It had been some time since Marthe had lost herself in me and my frog, though she had courted us and had her way with us through so many days and nights that I had come to believe that her passion for Armand would never die. But die it did, as I discovered one cold morning when accidentally I joined the pathetic little crowd of peasants in that village church. Even my mysterious Marthe was not immune to the rituals of conventional life, and so doomed herself there at the altar just as certainly my own Maman had doomed herself before that same cross and unconvincing priest. No sooner had Marthe uttered her vows, in a voice that I could not hear for its softness and the breathing of the peasants half filling that cold church, than I realized that Marthe too would one day resort to some pharmacist like our own Monsieur Remi, since poor Christophe's mother had herself been a child bride and only the most trusting of young females eventually resort to poison.

Of course dear Maman and Marie-Claude were trusting. After all, my mother had Papa, who was poison enough for any innocent bride and wife, while Marie-Claude escaped the stranglehold of convention soon enough, thanks to her vivacious nature.

But how or why did Marthe follow me that day from the church so long ago? Simply because, as I finally understood, I had long been legendary in Saint-Mamès, though that state of affairs hardly remained uppermost in my mind. As legendary as Saint-Mamès among the nuns. In fact, might I not have been as much the saint as Saint-Mamès? Pascal a saint? Who is to say that the true saint might not remain as skeptical as I have been since birth? He who is proclaimed a saint need hardly believe in sainthood.

Once Marthe disappeared from my life, so did Saint-

Mamès—in a paradoxical moment I recall with aston-
ishment to this day. Marthe gave me the statue of
Saint-Mamès, while Papa, in a sense, caused me to topple
him. That is, on still another afternoon or morning I
awoke from nothingness—as I continued to do occasionally from my idyllic childhood down through the false
chronology of my aging and still do—to find myself kneeling before Saint-Mamès, as I mentioned earlier. Yes, kneeling before the only saint with whom I have ever felt a
kinship, except that the pedestal on which he had stood,
for how many years of chanting and sanctity I do not
know, lay on its side as if some vandal had slipped among
us in the night to do his violence and flee. And the
wooden statue of my homely saint? Fallen also, half concealed in sharp grasses and wildflowers. I awoke of a sudden, stunned, kneeling on cold stones and captivated by
the look on the face of Saint-Mamès where he lay regard-
ing me from his ignoble position on the ground. I was
aware of nothing except the soulful expression that simply
obliterated any consciousness I might have had of my di-
shevelment, the scratches on my arms and face, the cold
that had all but impounded my flesh and blood on this
bright afternoon or morning, whichever it was. Aware
only, then, of the violation.

Naturally it took me but another few shallow breaths
to identify the villain. Myself, as anyone will have already
guessed. And the effect of this sudden, almost instanta-
neous blast of self-recognition? Terror, once more. Not
guilt, not self-defensiveness, not bafflement or denial, but

terror. After all, I may not be religious, but I am certainly not immune to superstition. Thus long after Armand had struck down Papa once and for all, so I irrevocably toppled the only saint—or at least his image—who might have relieved me of my sometimes crippling pain. Why irrevocably? Because if the wooden figure was relatively small and no doubt easy to lift and carry and replace atop his pedestal, so that what I had done might go unseen by anyone else who might stumble upon this overgrown corner of our asylum, nonetheless I did not touch him. And why did I not replace that saint and thus sweep from mortal sight at least any sign of my crime? Simply because the pedestal on which he had stood was far too heavy for any man or boy to lift. It had been carved of stone, its circumference was so great that I could not have clasped my arms around it, while its base was still larger around, as was the capital on which Saint-Mamès had stood. I might add that this capital had received all the ancient artisan's gold decorations that the saint himself had been spared. Well, then, I could hardly lift upright the column I had pushed off balance and sent crashing to the overgrown resting place where no doubt it lies to this day. A perfect illustration of cause and effect? Another unworthy comment that deserves no answer. But might not the terror I felt for the fall of the saint have been the exact same terror that I did not feel in having shared in causing the death of Papa? Not at all, though it is perfectly true that Saint-Mamès was another example of how the circumstances of my life conveniently repeated the essential opposites of my desire, evinced in my fixation on Maman on the one hand and Papa on the other.

So it was that thanks to Marthe I discovered Madame Chapôte or she discovered me, whichever you will, since in terror at what I had done, albeit unwittingly, in that dead lack of consciousness that I thought peculiar to myself, I rose to my feet as swiftly as I was able and fled the scene, disheveled and bleeding as I have said, and crashing blindly through thorny brambles without any sense at all of direction.

I emerged from the madness of untended nature precisely in time to hear the madness of the ringing bell—klaxon! alarm! all tumultuous warning sounds in one!—affixed to the handlebars of Madame Chapôte's bicycle, and to see her loom before me on the path onto which I had stumbled, and swerve, skirts flying, and go down. What a sight I must have been with my squat body, my scratched and profusely bleeding face and hands, my lips drawn widely up and back in my new state of shock.

"Oh, you poor thing," said Madame Chapôte— Marie-Claude—as she untangled herself from her voluminous skirts and lean black bicycle, the sight of me stifling the laugh with which she ordinarily met whatever events befell her. Afraid of me? Not at all, as her compassionate words made clear. And have you noticed by now how Marie-Claude's compound given name includes nothing less than the given name of my mother? Marie? No matter the extreme difference between Dr. Chapôte's wife and my mother, still they had their good natures in common as well as their names. At least Marie-Claude suited me in every way after our first superbly accidental meeting, from which her bicycle emerged unharmed, as did she, which did not prevent her from walking beside me the long way back to the populated heart of Saint-Mamès. She walked and talked, her thick pile of hair loosening atop her head with her every step and her volubility feeding both the shape and the animation of her haunches.

I see her still, wheeling the bicycle with one hand and holding high the front of her skirts with the other, looking up at me the while with amber-colored eyes, the energy of her smiling face so emphatic as to cause a faint perspiration on her upper lip. What would I have done without Marie-Claude? That kind woman took me into her home, in a manner of speaking, and eventually insisted that her husband, Dr. Chapôte, give me at least a modicum of his own attention, which, I can assure you, he bestowed on few indeed of our ever swelling numbers.

Thanks to little Marthe, as I say, I acquired the doctor's wife. Thanks to Marie-Claude I at last became her husband's most engaging patient, until he disabused me once and for all of gullibility. And thanks to Dr. Chapôte's small-mindedness I became the ward of Madame Fromage and in that capacity both protected and enjoyed the women who were as much the inmates of her establishment as I had been—and still am—an inmate of Saint-Mamès, no matter how privileged. Of course it was all my own doing, or Armand's. On the other hand, I must say at once that I did not hasten into what became a mutual captivity with Marie-Claude—or mutual freedom!—because of my legendary fame in Saint-Mamès or because of a few cuts and bruises and Marie-Claude's fall from her bicycle, though these contributed to our union. No, it was thanks to my culinary abilities that Marie-Claude gave me free rein of both her kitchen and her bedchamber. It did not take long for that lighthearted, passionate woman to catch me pausing in helpless admiration of this gleaming pot or that shining kettle hung readily to hand near the great stove that so resembled my mother's. Yes, once I had been introduced into Marie-Claude's kitchen I was like someone trapped in a museum by this or that gleaming canvas from which stepped pink ladies as lithe and carefree as children. Soon we were preparing tasty diminutive desserts together—I was an excellent pastry chef as well as master of soups and entrées, like my mother before me—and then the pâtés of ox tongue and the joints of mutton and asparagus ragouts that so naturally followed. Apparently Marie-Claude found my haunches as astonishing as I found hers, for in our culinary courtship her floured hand increasingly slipped to hold or stroke me, as my hand did her, without for a moment acknowledging that we had strayed from the actions and concentration strictly required by cooking. There was a great deal of laughing and bumping as I made my country duck or *omelettes Célestines,* which are two omelets, one within the other, each with a different filling and, in the oven, glazed like the portraits from which step the delicious ladies.

Precious, you say? Ah, but that too is a matter of opinion. And what young man is beyond such indulgences in the early flush of being the recipient of a woman such as Marie-Claude? I was not a seducer, and despite my initial experiences in the line of which we speak, I too was vulnerable in this way to such outright attentions paid me by a grown and married woman who was, after all, the wife of the man who had sole authority over the world in which I lived.

As for Dr. Chapôte himself, he could not believe the change that had overcome his table. How had his own wife discovered such shocking, delightful skills within herself, he asked happily while savoring the aromas of his wineglass and stuffing his overly small mouth with tastes of delectable dishes more mine than hers, as she reported back to me. Until that day long in coming when finally she deemed it safe to explode the ruse and to reveal the identity of the chef she had so long concealed in her kitchen—a young man of subtle disfigurement and warped perceptions who might have remained unknown amongst the so-called patients of Saint-Mamès had it not been for the merest stroke of mixed fortune that had befallen the doctor's wife one rainy day.

"But he's a genius!" Dr. Chapôte had cried, as Marie-Claude reported back to me. Her husband, as Marie-Claude told me in our garden, flowering with heat and steam and the smells of my stuffed pike, had succumbed entirely to the delectables with which I had outdone myself. But he had drawn the line at giving me the benefit of the training for which he was so well known, as Marie-Claude whispered to me one afternoon while puckering her lips and sucking on her first finger, which she had dipped into the sauce in which floated my lamb kidneys sautéed with garlic and morel mushrooms. After all, had said the doctor, was he to present to his colleagues a patient whose dementia resulted in *haute cuisine?* Why, said the doctor, the discussions would inevitably turn to cooking, and he would find himself the laughingstock of his profession.

But Madame Chapôte had insisted and, in her bland, ebullient manner, which her husband did not at all appreciate, had finally confronted him with the obvious threat, the outcome being that I was to appear before her husband, who, she warned me, was a man without feeling, despite his new and unseemly dining habits, who would no doubt insult the very idea of my frog, if I so much as mentioned Armand's existence. So I met Dr. Chapôte face-to-face, though I had no desire to do so and complied with Marie-Claude's wishes only because I wanted to please her in every way I could. Imagine my amazement, then, to find myself confronted by a geniality and even belief—yes, belief!—opposite that which Marie-Claude had given me to expect from her warning. For once she was wrong, or so it seemed, as happily I cringed before

Dr. Chapôte at his table and meal by meal allowed my fondling of Marie-Claude, and hers of me, to reach the bounds beyond which we certainly would go, and did.

"Gentlemen," said Dr. Chapôte in a quiet, jovial manner that quite surprised me out of my uncooperative mood, for it was one thing to be in that man's own home and another to appear submissive in the hospital setting I had been promised. "Gentlemen, we have before us a young man possessed by a frog—yes, gentlemen, a living frog!—whose habitat is our young man's stomach. It is quite the most unusual case of my career!"

How foolishly I grinned! How relieved I was, how filled with pride! Why, the very setting of my first interview with Dr. Chapôte was conducive to suspicion and that antagonism it conceals. We were in a small, cold stone amphitheater—all those white-coated colleagues of Dr. Chapôte, and the doctor himself, and I on my wooden chair in the middle and surrounded by their impassive or at best contemplative faces. They the physicians, I the patient. Why, I might as well have been a criminal! And the smoke? Yes, every last one of those white-coated figures, including Dr. Chapôte himself, was a pipe smoker. From that array of briar and meerschaum pipes, according to the size of their bowls and the vehemence with which those smokers puffed, came great clouds of smoke that contributed, as well they might have, to my initial anger and intimidation. Papa with his pipe, of course, and multiplied by twenty or so, with matches flaring and long self-satisfied blasts of smoke smothering the very breath in my lungs and thoughts in my brain, as well as burning my eyes. No matter my attachment to Marie-Claude, no matter how, according to her, I had already caused such a humanizing change in her husband, no matter how he had flattered me with praise of my cooking, still I was in no mood to trust that man, especially surrounded by such a battery of corpulent, white-coated skeptics. If Papa had tried to rid me of Armand, as indeed he had, what might not the chief administrator of Saint-Mamès and his colleagues—fathers, all of them—have had in store for my poor frog and hence for me as well? How, in their eyes, could my frog be anything but a delusion to be ridiculed and then dispelled by one odious means or another?

Not so! Not so at all!

"Gentlemen . . . ," the chief administrator of Saint-Mamès had said, and with those words and a friendly gesture in my direction had rid me of my slightest fear and acknowledged what I expected and demanded humankind to acknowledge—my credibility. What more could I want? But in so surprising me and causing me to reveal my childish pleasure, surely that sinister doctor, in all his cleverness, had relied on my naïveté to preserve my culinary compliance within his household and yet, at the same time, to make of my poor Armand a preposterous mockery. Did I not see that he was winking between puffs on his despicable pipe and, still further at my expense, making lewd facial expressions for the amusement of the audience, which could hardly contain itself? Oh, flattery of one sort or another is a cruel deceiver, and I was deceived. I should have known better, naïve or not. His tight smile, his prim clothing and high white collar and purple tie, his little black shoes and the white cuffs protruding from the sleeves of his jacket, the small, black, darting eyes that belied his smile—surely I should have known that my initial judgment of Dr. Chapôte was more than justified and that his jovial manner was but the emptiest obverse of his wife's good nature. He was a smiling hypocrite. And to think that that evening, still swollen with surprise and pride, I treated him to a pheasant pie with truffles!

Thus it was that periodically Lulu sought me out from amongst my less fortunate brothers and accompanied me to the amphitheater, where the air would already be impassable with pipe smoke and, behind his desk, Marie-Claude's husband would already be addressing his attentive colleagues. He was younger than they and shorter and of slighter build. Much slighter. Doll-like, in fact, despite his exalted position at Saint-Mamès. Inevitably my entrance interrupted his discourse. Inevitably my entrance was an intrusion on one disquisition or another. But let me just appear in their midst, dwarfed by the gentle Lulu, and Dr. Chapôte would stop in midsentence, lean back in his chair, and welcome me with his fatherly: "Why, look, gentlemen, it is none other than our young Pascal. And how is our frog today, young friend?" Oh, it was flattery heaped on flattery, yet never enough to hold my attention through all the long seasons that separated my visits to that sanctuary of medical science. Sometimes I found myself consciously awaiting my next beckoning to join the doctors and to hear the false heartiness in that thin voice —"See there, gentlemen, he is improving!"—though generally Lulu's summons came as a surprise that without warning threw showers of beatific light on my indolence. In everything he said, in every question he asked about Armand, I heard only approval. And all the while that man, who might have been considered frail had it not been for the harsh ligaments visible in his face, his neck, his hands, was beginning to test the limits of his tight clothing, thanks to—oh, but I need not say the obvious.

"Come in, come in, Pascal. . . . Gentlemen, I shall have more to say about Kraepelin another time. . . . And how is our frog? Thriving?"

Indeed he was. In fact during all those comforting scenes, when I was either displaying my art in Marie-Claude's kitchen or calling to mind bright images of the bric-a-brac that adorned her dressing table or of the immense lace skirt that shaded the chandelier in her dining room, I not only was free of even the occasional painful reminder of Armand's sometimes wicked existence but was generally spared any thought at all of my miraculous frog, so obsessed was I with Marie-Claude, and she with me. This so firmly womanly creature expressed no interest in seeing Armand or discussing him, as if she had quite forgotten that which made me legendary in Saint-Mamès or as if she wished no more of me than myself. Apparently my audacious Armand assumed that what Marie-Claude felt for me she also felt for him or because of him, which, though it was a pridefully wrong assumption, was just as well. Even a frog may be deluded by self-love. But wasn't that frog of mine our undoing? He was. Oh, he was!

For unbeknownst to either me or Marie-Claude, he had in fact worked his silent way into my companion's mind and there lay feasting on her unadmitted cravings as greedily as he feasted on the very tissues and liquids of my being. Yes, he caught my Marie-Claude quite un-awares, though gradually, slowly working his insidious ac-tuality to the fore as increasingly she became more girlish, more prone to flushing, quicker to seize my hand and draw me onward, ever closer to the relics and fabrics that were totems, so to speak, of all that amounted to her sacred privacy. In other words she changed from the un-selfconscious woman that until now she had shown herself to be, to a woman who helplessly cloaked her bodily heat in a shyness that cried aloud for rending. Yes, my forth-right Marie-Claude was losing her common sense, her sim-ple boldness of person, her honest laughter. Yes, she was on the verge of deceiving us both, and her husband as well, thanks to my merciless frog and though we had not the slightest warning of what lay ahead.

"We interviewed him again today, Marie-Claude. He

was wonderful! Wonderful! Even old Dr. Dampierre admits he is quite a find. And to think that he can prepare *daube de poussin* as heavenly as this!"

We too—Marie-Claude and I—were growing plump, though not on my cooking. And all the while the night of my frog was approaching. Until it arrived as, had I only known, it must.

One early evening, you see, Marie-Claude suddenly begged me to quit her kitchen for, as she put it, a moment only and to accompany her into the silken darkness that was her own. I demurred—my casserole was on the stove—yet submitted against my will to her urgency. And Armand? Oh yes, Armand was stirring about inside me, making himself known again as he had not for longer than I could remember, and readying himself, as I could feel, with the rankest kind of anticipation.

Beware, Pascal!

But there in the darkness, and still wearing my white apron stained with blood and the residue of spilled gravies, I did not heed that warning. Quite the opposite, for whatever bright frenzy had finally overcome Marie-Claude, a glimmer of which was beginning to dawn in my stomach, I could not disappoint the woman whose every need, or so I thought, I had already filled. It was the wrong hour, you see, a dangerous hour. Below us the doctor's favorite dish of eels was beckoning me back to my fiery stove. Good judgment was tugging on my apron. Oh, but Marie-Claude had drawn down the silken spread and lighted a candle in a silver holder wound with vines and bursting grapes. What she had bared of herself with fingers too cold and trembling to cope with that feminine array of hooks and snaps was also bursting. My nose was assaulted by the precious scent of the eels, the flame of the candle was plump with the orange light in which we bathed.

"Pascal," she murmured from where she lay languishing in that soft light, "please . . ."

Well, I knew what she wanted. Naturally those two words were Armand's cue. Slowly he began his journey upward, helplessly I waited to lend him my assistance. But up he came, quite as if he had no need of me at all, and so enjoying his tantalizing progress that he lengthened it in a manner new to us both, so slowly stretching himself that his webbed feet remained in my stomach even as his eager head parted my lips and surveyed the prostrate woman who by all rights should have been entirely mine. Oh, but he was preparing for a performance, was my Armand, already of such an elastic slithering length that he might have been one of the doctor's golden eels. He was immense, though still lodged from top to bottom within me. He was electric with the attention he was about to receive. In my mouth his head was beginning to swell as if in delighted sympathetic response to the uncovered bosom on which he cast his prideful eyes.

"Pascal," whispered Marie-Claude. "Hurry, Pascal. . . ."

I must admit that now, despite myself, I was once

more as proud of Armand as he was of himself. He was mine, after all, the only such frog in existence, as far as I knew, the source of my worst pain and a power that exceeded manhood. I had seen the horror he had inspired in my father's eyes, I had been the only witness to the ways in which little Marthe had succumbed to him. But here, now, was Marie-Claude, a mature woman already brought low by my Armand, and he had not even fully emerged from my mouth. It was no wonder, then, that I forgot myself as well as the drama playing itself out on the stove below.

Gently I contracted my abdominal muscles, opened my mouth to its fullest, gently assisted the disgorgement of my now shockingly immense frog bent on wooing. With thumb and forefinger I seized him under the arms, as I cannot help but call them, though in fact he was possessed of but one such limb intact and the mere stump of the other, and drew him forth, which was a matter so prolonged, so amazing, that I might have been extracting from myself some inordinate length of my own vital organs. Indeed, perhaps by now my frog had in fact become one of my vital organs, though clearly I was only his convenience and he his own frog.

But there in the candlelight and from my gentle fingers he hung, great flaccid creature glistening quite as if he had been freshly dipped in melted butter, his limbs loose, his golden breast as large as my palm. His head drooped, the better to see Marie-Claude, no doubt, and the smell he emitted was not his usual smell of the ancient frog pond but of the butter with which he appeared to be dripping. The candle cast his elongated shadow on Marie-Claude's nude bosom, one of his distended legs twitched in delight at what he saw. He was heavy, dangling there from my fingers.

"Pascal," she finally managed to whisper, "he is glorious! . . ."

But what voice was that? What voice that answered? Exactly. Exactly.

"Marie-Claude!" came the angry, strangled cry from below. "Where are you? What is the meaning of this? The eels are burning!"

And so they were. But I must admit here and now that the doctor's untimely return—how could Marie-Claude have so flouted the hour and subjected me to the wrath of that little man quivering below in the darkness? —paralyzed me with terror so thick, so black, that it filled the very mouth and stomach only moments before occupied by my preening frog. I dropped him. I watched him sprawl on Marie-Claude's heaving bosom. And then I ran, clumsily but swiftly, beating my retreat from the scene of my guilt as once I fled the boudoir of the young count's wife. Without a thought to Armand or Marie-Claude I quit her chamber and clattered down the servants' staircase and out into the night that rang with shouts and cries as if it took only my running person to start my fellow inmates howling, much as one barking dog sets off the barking of every other dog for villages and farms around.

It was raining. I was bareheaded. My apron flapped, my teeth were clenched.

But Armand! What of Armand? I had left him! I had abandoned him! Exactly what I had feared would come to pass—the loss of my frog—was now upon me. It was intolerable! But what did I hear then? Footsteps! The sound of running! Yes, that wretched little doctor was giving chase, running bareheaded in my pursuit quite indistinguishable from one frenzied inmate or another dashing in circles on that rainy night. Well, no terror was strong enough to deprive me forever of my lascivious frog. And could Armand actually live without me? He could not. Of course he could not.

So clumsily I doubled back and retraced my steps, entered the darkened corridor I had just fled, and found my way to Marie-Claude's silken chamber.

"Armand!" I cried. "Where is he?"

But I might have spared myself the slightest worry. For there he sat, unperturbed, stately in the warm light of the candle, all but nestling in Marie-Claude's nakedness. I seized him, of course, roughly, indifferent to both the frog's surprise and Marie-Claude's alarm, and stuffed him back into my mouth and down my gullet where he belonged. And stealthily, this time, I returned to the rain and listened to the faint sounds of Dr. Chapôte still raging into this barred room or that.

Retribution? It was swift enough in coming, I can tell you. But not in any form I could have predicted. In fact I began to think that Armand and I might go unpunished after all, since I quite cheerfully refrained from paying my usual visits to Marie-Claude's kitchen and surmised, reasonably enough, that our medical director must surely be suffering from his sharpening hunger for those savory meals that no longer graced his table. Surely Marie-Claude would beckon me back to her stove and the doctor overlook my little transgression for the sake of my cooking. So I waited, my confidence returning, and Armand kept himself as still as a mouse.

But the only person who sought me out, at last, was the hulking Lulu, who, sunk in atypical glumness, summoned me, one gray day, for what proved to be my final scrutiny by the white-coated patriarchal doctors. I had come to enjoy their attention along with the authentication I was by now used to receiving from Dr. Chapôte. Never once did it occur to me to expect anything different. That our medical director was quite capable of stooping to use this medical forum for his own purposes, or as a means of airing his petty, personal wrath, could not have been farther from my mind.

Wrong again, Pascal. Beware.

"Gentlemen," he said, his pipe unlit, his face drawn, "it is time to call a spade a spade. Or perhaps I should say a frog a frog." He smiled grimly at his little joke and then spoke on, barely containing his malice in the startling remoteness of his youthful face. "If you will recall, gentlemen, it is to the great Emil Kraepelin that we owe our knowledge of *dementia praecox* and manic-depressive psychosis. The patient before us is a classic case of the former. Beyond a doubt. Gentlemen, the frog whose virtues he has extolled at length does not exist. There is no frog! However, gentlemen, I assure you that this patient is harmless. The world has nothing to fear from the little green amphibian which has no reality except in the patient's own warped mind. So let me repeat, gentlemen—the so-called Armand is a delusion, as described by the great Kraepelin, of which we have heard enough. Enough! We shall have no more humoring of this foolish frog!"

Does not exist? Delusion? Warped mind? Oh, suffice it to say that there I sat, stunned, denounced, and humiliated before the entire gravely nodding lot of them. Was it possible that this Dr. Chapôte—Marie-Claude's white-faced husband—considered me as much his betrayer as he was mine? Could he have been driven to a revenge as unwarranted as this? Apparently so.

Some such understanding, or rather incomprehension, blurred my sight, filled my head with the crashing of the blackest sea. I grew as red in the face as an open wound. I began to swell with the inexpressible. I grew cold. I hovered on the brink of self-abasement. Then, at last, I was seized by a fit of trembling grander than any I had ever known, even in that worst moment of my childhood. In fact I trembled so fiercely that I could not move, though it was clear to all that had I been able to, I would have rushed at that little man and treated him to the brute strength of my bare hands. Yet I could not take so much as a step, toward him or away. It was the violence of pure paralysis. Can you imagine? Finally it was thanks only to Lulu that I did not tear myself apart, fiber by fiber, in the midst of my terrible trembling, with which in fact I longed only to assault my benefactor turned persecutor, for my great kind attendant simply picked me up bodily, as if I had still been the child Pascal, and with the greatest tenderness carried me from that scene of my worst disgrace. But not before I saw over Lulu's shoulder Marie-Claude's husband calmly lighting his pipe.

But was he puffing away in self-satisfaction only because he had unmasked my frog, as he thought? Hardly. Not at all. For the treachery of our medical director finally assumed the simplest form but one that nonetheless swept me up in a hurt more painful than the humiliation into which he had plunged Armand and me. He wanted me gone. He enlisted Lulu—poor, well-meaning Lulu—to rid Saint-Mamès of my presence and to escort me out of our medical director's mind forever. No risk of discovering young Pascal in his kitchen or otherwise. No more jealousy for Dr. Chapôte. Or so he thought.

A cardboard suitcase, a forlorn overcoat and hat, the hulking Lulu, and the train in which I rode off alone— or nearly alone. And my surprise, my bewilderment, my grief. But what we did not know—the illustrious Dr. Chapôte and I—was that Marie-Claude had already thrown herself, so to speak, on Bocage. And that on the very day that Lulu was pinning the address of my destination to my lapel, Bocage was secretly carrying off the doctor's wife. Yes, the doctor's wife.

Oh, Marie-Claude, I cannot live without you!

❃✻❃

CHAPTER THREE

Madame Fromage

I HAVE SEEN THAT ALREADY! I cry out. *I have done that before!* Which is to say that periodically I recognize what I have never seen and remember some insignificant or momentous event even as it occurs for the first time. For me your ordinary *déjà vu* is like being hit by a train. You see, I cannot bear being the victim of what only appears impossible. Give me what is truly impossible or leave me alone. Surely I need not add that what I have just described does not contradict the ravages of my so-called fits, when I awaken, so to speak, to the terror of a world gone utterly unfamiliar. Being lost is nothing compared to the effect of my fits or my rage at such uncontrollable self-deceptions.

Complaining? I am not complaining, which you would know if you had been listening. For instance, Papa was a complainer. But not I.

Well, then, that train I have just mentioned crept into our lowly, provincial station as if to tear it down. The massive locomotive, an inferno clad in iron, was heavily cloaked with the same soot and cinders with which it all but obliterated the station and blinded Lulu and me, like black snow. What dark sulfurous magnificence! As for the passenger cars in its tow, how they clanked and rattled, their windows blackened as much by the distances through which they had been dragged as by the soot, the cinders.

The blind man and the cripple? Of course they were aboard that train, though I was too preoccupied with my own grief and consternation to catch sight of them, except at my journey's end. Furthermore, the noise of that locomotive was as deafening as it was blinding, while the confusion inherent in the way it shook the station where we waited, Lulu and I, was certainly a match for the inner confusion into which Armand and I had been so abruptly cast. There was no reason for our apparent banishment from Saint-Mamès, since at that moment I had not the slightest idea that Marie-Claude had already forsaken the place forever. Then too, I never thought of myself as a traveler, and there beside the wonderfully intimidating mass of the locomotive, I could not have been more ill at ease with shabby hat, threadbare overcoat, and hollow near-empty suitcase. Was I not going forth as the worst kind of pretender? So I thought.

My age at the beginning of this journey? Of course the simplest arithmetic will reveal both the sorry state of the nation—our nation—into which I was venturing, as well as my age at the time. A child could do that calculation. Yet if even a glimpse of our national troubles crossed my mind at that moment—imagine an entire nation of barred doors and shuttered windows, which was the spirit of those times if not the fact—I probably told myself that all those countrymen of ours deserved no better. Wait now! Restrain yourself! No matter the rashness of what I say—as it may seem to you—I did my part, as did Armand, though given what you have heard so far, you will be the first to admit that I have no use for valor. None at all. I may even go so far as to say that I prefer cowards to heroes, given a choice. But make no mistake, I love what I mock. As for my moment of national service, as I shall call it, it is yet to come, as you of course shall see.

Then that waiting train was gone and I had taken my sorry seat within, alone in an empty compartment with the soot, the cinders, which, if anything, were thicker, blacker, more acrid inside than out. Already my nostrils were blackened, my loose clothing stiffened with that dark grit. I sat bolt upright, clutching my battered suitcase to my side, and allowed the ill-shapen hat to remain where it was on my head. We were moving! The seat beneath me swayed and jerked according to the simplemindedness of that hunching locomotive fit for a child. I smiled, without letting down my guard, of course, since no matter what I had said or thought, I was a traveler, despite myself. A traveler!

Au revoir, Lulu.

Iron to iron. Shriek to silence. Away we went. On the seat facing mine the pages of an open book, abandoned, apparently, by the last person to occupy my compartment, turned themselves now left, now right, fanning erratically as if no reader would ever again retrieve that book. I was alone. Outside my rattling window the green countryside was black with soot. Not a hovel, not a peasant, not even a chicken nosing through the cinders. Back and forth went the untouched pages; the unbearable heat of the locomotive filled the air. Where were we going? Why? Suddenly, in the strange motion of my solitude, I understood the pleasure of the blind man and the cripple.

But whether or not I was truly alone, as the couplings banged and the train went on, is a moot point. For once, driven into the corridor, I glanced between the curtains of the compartment adjoining mine, and there, beyond the curtained glass and propped between the facing seats, was a slender silver coffin with a few pale roses strewn on its lid.

Dear Maman. To think that we should be traveling on the same train!

Well, like the boy I had temporarily become, I was not able to stay away from my own compartment window for long, and so, despite the roses trembling to the exact same motion as the pages of that unread book I have already described, and despite the terrible and totally feminine attraction of that silvery casket, I returned to my seat, once again clutching to my side that hollow-sounding valise and thinking to reassure myself that my rumpled hat was yet firmly in place, as it was.

The few meager cows we now passed inevitably turned their backs to us, as did the horses—how profound the humiliation of our sad country!—and, as I could see, were

already drenched in soot before my train approached, so
that the soot and cinders of my locomotive were one thing
and those of the countryside another, and the result of a
source vaster indeed than the flames that burned in the
firebox of my iron engine. As for the air both inside and
outside this train, how pleased I was by the rotten, cordite
smell that was so unavoidable to human and animal
breathing alike. The stink of the train already out of sight,
how I sucked it in, no matter my rigidity on the edge of
my seat.

The title of the abandoned book whose pages still
swung to and fro like undulating fronds of seaweed in a
dead sea? Why, it never occurred to me to look. In fact,
I would not have disturbed those unread pages for the
world. I am sure that they are even now beating pointlessly
to the rhythm of my fierce, clumsy train, in themselves a
death of sorts, due all respect.

How curious that it took only the first signs of the
modest, impoverished city that was of course our destination for our speed to decrease and the locomotive to
exert itself, to labor as it had not even when the length of
our journey had been most demanding, as if the closer we
drew to that surprisingly private city, despite its former
enterprise and now unseen population, the more it exerted
itself, in a sort of inverse magnetism, to prevent our crawl-
ing into its empty terminal, which, had it not been for a
final slow surging of our engine, it might have done. But
to have ridden that long way without having had so much
as a glimpse of the blind man and the cripple I have in-

sisted were on the same train? Oh, but I did in fact catch sight of them, when, in growing bewilderment, I found myself on that pocked and empty station platform and turned, clutching my hat to my head but forgetting my suitcase, and saw the two of them far ahead of me, tiny figures happily walking side by side. How did I recognize that energetic pair? By the two crutches and the single white cane that propelled them alone. How else?

Well, beyond the rails and wires and cinders and soot—or rather into a city of cinders and soot—eventually I began to make my solitary way down tiny streets and wide avenues lined with shops and houses with their eyes sealed shut by this hasty barricade or that. Already I missed the safety of my railway train compartment, though I did not upbraid myself for the loss of my suitcase, which had joined my somehow missing destination tag as well as the abandoned book to further beguile the next solitary passenger to board that train. Of course the streets were not entirely empty, for now and again I quite sensibly stepped aside to allow the passing of those hulking figures in black boots and uniforms who, in twos and threes, came down the sidewalks shoulder to shoulder, their black rumps swinging high and their heads in visored black caps tilted imperiously upwards so that they might see their way. What a clatter they made, how swiftly they went! Why, they might have been growling and snarling had it not been for their human eyes and faces, as they pursued their frightening progress.

Armand? Of course I have not forgotten Armand. It

was quite beyond my control that Armand chose to curl himself into an innocuous ball, a tiny philosopher's stone in my stomach, as soon as the immensity of our dislocation became apparent, and only now, in the emptiness of these streets and alleys in which I was lost, began to loosen himself and to flex himself, inspired by a sudden interest in this guarded place, as if he could see these vistas of cobblestones and hanging wires and the occasional wall forever scarred by some brief and swiftly ended ambush or assassination, though he could not.

Let me repeat that however singular the episodes I may recount, my two primary concerns still remain my frog and my mother, though affliction in general and women in general obsess me as much, I believe, as Papa. Now we come to women in another dimension.

To think that they were expecting me! And how different they were from the several wives who, until this moment, had led me into what I learned of my own manhood, despite my distaste for the male attributes. The unmarried woman, you see, is quite unlike your widow, for instance, or that person who is in fact the wife of a living man. On the one hand, she who is not the victim of religious union offers no stimulation through the promise of transgression, while on the other hand, your wife or widow is generally obscured, no matter how faintly, by her dead or living husband's shadow. Of course she whose husband has died by her own hand is a different matter altogether, and as far as I know not one of Madame Fromage's women had ever resorted to poison. But come to think of it, that sweet young person known as Placide was in fact married, and to a singing master who sometimes visited Madame Fromage's hotel to give his own wife or one of the other girls, as they were known among themselves, those singing lessons at which he was quite adept —which, I suppose, destroys my argument. But remember my scorn for the so-called airtight argument!

How could I possibly have found them, those four young women wed in a sense to their work, without my scrap of paper and with no one to read it even if it had still been pinned in place to my lapel? By smell, of course. Not by the telltale scent of gardenia or jasmine or that of some other raw perfume—though Placide and the other three managed to get hold of small vials of these trite hallmarks of arousal, no matter the scarcity of even bread in this city, with its soot and suspicion and despair—but by the smell of cooking. Yes, cooking, no matter that what I smelled cooking was scarcer by far than bread.

Here I should say that throughout my life with Armand so far, I had adhered to the diet I had prescribed for myself as a child, depriving myself of the *haute cuisine* I had prepared for the only jealous husband I had ever known, except for a taste here, a sip there, as required by the cooking itself. But I could smell! Indeed I tuned the flavors more by smell than taste—I, a man of the senses! And one who denied himself wine for water! Depriving myself to spare Armand the discomfort, or worse, of various fats and acids, which I suppose it all comes down to. How many fields of grain did I force myself to eat for the sake of my frog? How great my dislike of those pallid grains, how great my sacrifice for a frog no doubt thriving yet languishing for white insects!

But all at once, then, there on that apparently empty street, I smelled an impossible aroma. *Rognons.* Kidneys. Of an infant lamb, no less. *Rognons d'agneau.* Could it be? I stopped, I faced the walls of all that I had been so heedlessly passing. And suddenly, looking closer, widening my nostrils and breathing as deeply as I could, I found the source of what was cooking on that invisible greasy stove. Why, at that time, as I might say in retrospect, a person could be put to death for less than having clandestinely procured a food so scarce as to be strictly forbidden to our population at large.

Yet there it was. A *bistro.* With metal shutters drawn down and thus protecting the glass window they surely hid, and a door with a shade drawn meanly behind the square of glass bearing the name of the place painted in letters so faded as to be all but illegible. And hanging in this doorway, between shade and dismal glass, a sign. *Fermé.* But obviously this little place of nourishment was not closed, since the aroma it managed to emit was strong enough to lure at the run every gaunt dog in this city, had they not already been destroyed for the sake of our hungry children. How could I not enter that *bistro,* the likes of which I had never seen? I, a chef? I, who had traveled all that long day on that train without so much as a cheese in my pocket?

Inconsistent? But you know already that I am not the

sort to assume responsibility for my inconsistencies. Oh, I glory in inconsistencies, as you know full well.

Inside were two women, one young, one middle-aged, one quite ordinary in build and the other nearly half again as large and a perfect match for her great iron stove, which filled half of that small, claustrophobic room. Two tables, at one of which the young woman sat with her knees crossed, a short skirt pulled tight and midway up her naked thigh, and on her head a hat as shabby and shapeless as the one I still wore. And above all, butter—think of it!—and the hot skillet and the *rognons* cooking in a film of that butter over a high flame.

At that moment the vows I had once taken for Armand's sake, and to which I had been faithful my life long, were shattered. In an instant I made my determination. I would eat! Yes, eat! Eat what I wished! And so I sat down at the second table, so necessarily close to the other that the younger woman's half-bared thigh, which lay slightly flattened atop its twin since she had crossed her legs while waiting, was so close to me that only the thought of the *rognons* caused me to avert my eyes.

How am I able to comment in such detail on the legs on which I did not allow my eyes to dwell? But what did I say a mere instant ago about inconsistency? Visual lust and inconsistency make fine bedfellows, I can tell you. Of course it is a commonplace that a memory of a later time may color if not change entirely a former. No doubt you will give me that and, further, spare me your quibbling when I say that the young person sitting so close to me that I could smell the vivid wash of perspiration that burst from her armpits and vied with her cheap perfume and the aroma of the *rognons* on the stove and grease on the walls was none other than Placide herself. How I attempted to keep my eyes down, how compulsively she crossed and recrossed her legs, thus conveying unintentionally that one thigh was as good as the other—the left or right—as long as those thighs increasingly bared were hers. And that innocent face, I saw in a glance, was as glistening as must have been her armpits. On the small flat round of her table, almost as bare of utensils as mine, stood a by now only half-filled *carafe* of red wine and a *ballon,* with which she toasted me silently and with an embarrassed smile, though of course I was as yet without a similar *carafe* and *ballon* with which to reciprocate— except for the sudden and obviously unwanted smell of my own perspiration, inspired as much by Placide's mimed pleasantries and discomfort as by the heat of the place.

The *rognons* were filled inside with a liquid pinkness and a taste to match. The wine, which must have been smuggled into this city and this *bistro* from some soot-covered farm that appeared to be abandoned but was not, gave me to know with the first crude sip that the acidic redness now filling my mouth was identical to that filling Placide's own mouth, though of course I had yet to learn her name. We might as well have been kissing as eating and drinking there in the approving shadow of that immense woman who spoke our language, when she did so, in a fashion revealing that our own beautiful language was not natively hers, though I hasten to add that the way she spoke made plain that in every possible way she was distinct from those rude intruders from whom she managed to conceal her *bistro,* as if it was as dead and empty as the rest of the city appeared to be.

Monsieur?

Madame?

But to my everlasting good fortune it was Placide who thus addressed me, and not our immense provider, masked in incivility, and Placide who smiled unwittingly and at the same time laid a bare hand atop a bare thigh before the next abrupt recrossing of her legs played havoc with her hands, her knife and fork, her *ballon,* the point being twofold—Placide's natural modesty and natural desire went contrarily together, as I was to come to know, yet bathed that young woman in an irrepressible charm as distant as possible from that coyness to which so many of our females pretend, excluding, of course, the other three compatriots sheltered, like Placide, by Madame Fromage. The second point being that Placide was awaiting me there in that *bistro.* Think of it!

Yes, awaiting me—and me alone—in that forbidden eating place to which Madame Fromage certainly knew I would be lured—by the smell! the smell!—and passing the time with *rognons* sautéed in butter, mind you, and her *carafe* of red wine. Yes, my guide, though our journey together was only but one door away from the *bistro*'s, yet sent specifically to await me, find me, and take me to

Madame Fromage herself, as if that woman had prior knowledge that I would lose my identifying scrap of paper and that only hunger would overcome the fear and bewilderment in which I found myself lost in this ugly city. And though Placide, the first of Madame Fromage's women to set eyes on me, from the outset treated me exactly as if I were an adult male in search of a woman like Placide, nonetheless she saw the youth, if not the frog, buried deep inside me. Thus her nervousness was at least twofold, and thus, though I was hardly aware of it, I had no sooner sat down at that round table—a small, wobbling affair, I can tell you—than I had in fact reached the end of my journey.

Monsieur!

Madame!

Have I remarked that Lulu was Madame Fromage's nephew? Or that I was not the first person at Saint-Mamès deemed at last fit enough to take his place in the world at large? No? Well, even I am at a loss to account for my interest in these "reasons" that so brought to life my new circumstances, when in fact I have only the barest interest in either reasons or circumstances. As for Armand, he was doing his best to cripple me on the spot, thanks to the wine if not the *rognons,* so that even when Placide pushed back her chair and rose to her feet and extended her hand, I was in such pain that only my most unaccountable determination allowed me to seize that hand and to follow Placide—so near, so far—to what I naturally thought of as the place of my new employ. No doubt Placide mistook

the pains in my stomach for the ambivalence of any youthful man, for such I must have seemed to her, encountering
for the first time a woman such as herself. My barrel chest,
remember, promised strength beyond the ordinary, while
my ageless face was either frightening or endearing to
women—though rarely have I met a woman repelled by
me, any more than by Armand. Placide, I should add, was
the first to discover the erotic qualities of Armand—all
the more intense since found in a frog!—though I did not
intend to discriminate between the sisters, as they were
sometimes known, who, unlike myself, received each week
from Madame Fromage's grudging hand a handsome
number of *francs,* all of them worthless at that time, as
the world knows. Imagine that modest Placide indirectly
accepting money from her own husband, when it was he,
after all, who was the singing teacher!

Yes, I shall say it again. Modest! In fact so becomingly
modest that whether stark naked or fully clothed, if so
short a skirt does not belie my argument, she was likely
to spread one open hand starfish style flat in the middle
of her chest, thus hiding what no boy or man might have
wished to see. Imagine! Exposing her breasts while concealing her chest! I suppose that Placide would have been
my favorite, if I had indeed allowed myself to weigh one
against the other, which I did not.

As for Madame Fromage, such was not her christened
name—naturally not—though of course she was known
by that name because of her passion for cheese, which is
a feather in the cap of cause and effect, if such is your

inclination. For me, as you know, it is not the obvious connection between that woman's *nom de plume,* if I may so twist a figure of speech, and her eating habits that is of interest, but the euphony of the name on the one hand and, on the other, the pungency of her obsession, which, quickly enough, I came to share. Imagine Armand's suffering and, thanks to him, my own! What could have been a deadlier fare for a frog? And who was the crueler persecutor, Armand or Pascal? Perhaps we should just say that in the end it was a draw, since in torturing my stubborn frog I was at last savoring the sensualities of eating, while he, in furious retaliation, inflicted on me pain as never before and, for the first time, partook of a kind of eroticism usually reserved for humans, in the process giving himself new wind, so to speak, while sending my reputation with women to new heights. Thus the severity of our give-and-take, as if we were shouting at each other from opposite ends of a long plank balanced across an old milk churn tipped on its side. We were quite a pair, Pascal and Armand, though for Madame Fromage and the others my frog had not yet come into the picture.

Have I mentioned that Madame Fromage emitted a curious whistling from the side of her neck whenever she spoke? Well, so she did, thanks to an old injury or wound sustained at the hands of one of our medical practitioners. She might as well have had a tin whistle buried in that neck of hers. How proudly she defined her eccentric self with every smelly bite she took and every word she said! Need I add that impairment is more to my liking than good health? That a grim city is preferable to any pretty metropolis on a postcard? Yes, mine was and still is an aesthetic of contrariness. I will take a pile of rubble over a picturesque village any day, or a scorched landscape over a flowering one, since it promises all the more the greenness that once was and may yet come to be.

"How dazed he is, Placide. Oh, come in, come in, you poor creature."

Another stage, another chapter of my life, and as like the one to the other as a crooked thumb to its print. What were Madame Fromage and her four shadows if not variants of dear Maman? And who most brought to mind my one-legged father if not the owner of the black military cap occasionally hanging from one of the antlers of the imposing coat stand looming in a corner of our small foyer? As for the frog pond, that natural wonder from which I, in a sense, came into being, it too was duplicated in this time and place that denied once and for all the very thought of tree or cow. And what in this soot-covered tangle of wires and empty streets could so compel my attention as my frog pond once did? Why, my switchboard, of course, a glorious affair of dust and electrical sensibility and little mechanical plugs and holes that sat upright, commandingly, on a table behind the front desk, as it was called, behind which and beside which I stayed day in and out, beguiled by the power entrusted to me, as I thought, in the switchboard. It connected me to the women's rooms, a flashing light no larger than an aching tooth requiring me to pull this plug or that one and to push it, with utmost seriousness, into the socket now indicated by the sudden appeal of the small orange light. As soon as I heard the far-off voice of Placide or Bluette, or Verveine or Béatrice, the orange light extinguished itself like the pain that can no longer be remembered once the tooth is clenched in the child's fist. Yes, there I sat hour upon hour, concentrating on that ancient switchboard as if I were a chess player on a winter's day, until I saw one of the tiny lights and hastened to rearrange the requisite wires, and then listened intently to this woman's voice or that one, and then followed her orders. Of course I was as much in thralldom to that mechanical device, the more attentive to what it would demand of me the longer its silence lasted, as I had once been to my frog pond.

I soon discovered that I was not merely at the beck and call of Bluette or Béatrice, or of Placide or Verveine, but could, unbidden, employ my switchboard so as to listen, unbeknownst to them, to their small talk with this visitor or that. And when speech gave way to the rhythmic breathing and small cries or even angry groans that I never tired of overhearing? What a privilege! Not merely to carry out their requests, sharply conveyed or lazily, depending on their moods, but to amuse myself by spying, so to speak, on one encounter from start to finish, or by switching rapidly from room to room, mixing the words of one with the little screams of another, like a composer arranging not only the notes of a musical score but the audible intimacies of what no man should be allowed to hear, except as a participant. And do you know that I was never caught at my harmless violations of privacy? And that I most enjoyed listening to those sessions involving the music master and this swooning partner or that one? But of course!

"*Bonjour,* Monsieur de La Fayette."

"*Bonjour,* Pascal."

The music teacher, the small man with the big name and even more consumed with modesty than his modest wife, was to me the most captivating of all the clients who visited Madame Fromage's establishment. I could count on him, as no other, to proceed from words—his own— to actual singing—Placide attempting once again her scales—to a rare duet as his speech became halting and the formal lyricism of Placide's voice yielded to what no songwriter could even put on paper. Oh, how I felt like a lone man pressing his ear to a thin wall in a foreign hotel and listening to the pleasures enjoyed by some invisible pair on the other side but forever denied to the likes of him! Except that soon enough Placide and the others denied me nothing, as we would expect.

I undertook their errands, carrying to their various rooms trays of bread and sausage and the inevitable *carafes* of red wine, all of which had been readied for me in the *bistro,* or bringing them bottles of water or emptying their dirty basins or covering their bare shoulders with the silk of faded negligees. Under my ministrations, how quickly they recovered, how swiftly they revived, their bodies dried of the fatigue of the encounter just ended, their minds already quickening to the next. Sometimes I anticipated the languid messages I heard at my switchboard, and so appeared in their doorways unbidden, in time to see this or that happily puffing client pulling up his wrinkled trousers or to see Béatrice, for instance, poised at the beginning of her recovery, with or without my help, from the one-sided struggle in which she had only the moment past been entangled. Béatrice kneeling, half sitting on the stained carpeting at the foot of her still rumpled bed of sorts, her long black unwashed hair hiding her face, an unwelcome shadow hiding the single breast exposed to my view, one slim leg crossed upon the other as she braced herself with one hand on the mattress and one on the carpet, and turned to me most of all her buttocks, beyond which we shall have no indelicacies.

At such moments was I aware of myself as intruder? As somehow more accountable than the man so lately coarse or shy in leaving our Béatrice? I was. Of course I was. And yet when she or Verveine or Bluette finally turned her head and eyes in my direction, and smiled, it was not at all to pronounce, in silence, the guilt I felt on those unwitting occasions of mine but, in that same silence, to smile at me an unmistakable beckoning. *You too, Pascal? You too, perhaps?*

How rapid was my progress from open door to open arms!

One morning, when my story had all but slipped beyond the securities of time, I discovered in our dark foyer an empty perambulator, yet I caught neither sight nor sound of the person for whom that vehicle was intended.

There it was, for the morning only, a detail in a history that defies explanation, mine included. It had no significance, or all the significance you might impart to its empty interior. Pillow and blanket, in size befitting that missing infant, made that black perambulator all the more confounding. Did one of our four women have a dark secret? Did it belong to Madame Fromage herself, a relic of a different order of life? I confess it made me think of Maman and Papa, though as far as I know I never rode in a perambulator. Then again, the emptiness of that small machine, poised as it was on high springs, made me shudder and fight down a sudden vision of Armand himself proudly riding along a sylvan footpath on a summer's eve.

When again I passed through the foyer that day, the perambulator was gone, of course. But at my switchboard the lights were flashing and in fact my senses were so keyed to the promises that awaited me with Placide that I gave it hardly a thought.

And how did Placide—for it was she, as I have said —manage to introduce Armand to the activity that might have left him lifeless had I not intervened? Simple enough.

One afternoon—another—in my timeless round of afternoons and mornings of joining Madame Fromage for a tasting of hard cheese or soft, sweet or rancid, or of attending to the needs of her charges, as she in her whistling voice sometimes called them, and of surreptitiously studying the men who found their way into our underworld, I intruded on Placide engaged with an enormous client whom I had only moments before seen passing my front desk. They were all the same, those men, turning away their heavy faces and failing to acknowledge my greetings. At any rate, when I happened to open Placide's door, this citizen was still hiding his face between her open legs while she, still partially clothed, was propping her torso half upright and smiling at me—quite stripped of the modesty that had until this moment been her hallmark and charm.

I retreated. Soon the big fellow did the same, fixing his trousers even as he passed the front desk with wet face averted. There were no flashing lights. No errands. No distractions, except for Armand, who, his own passions or anger somehow aroused—could he see through my eyes? hear through my own ears?—was jabbing me here and there in my lower abdomen so that it was all I could do to prevent myself from gasping and doubling over. I kept to my place behind the front desk. Armand did not desist. My pain increased, as what color was left in my white face drained away. And then? Of course. In a corner of my otherwise dead dusty switchboard one light flashed. Placide. A summons that involved no more than taking myself and my livid frog up those unlighted stairs that were like the remnants of a snail's shell, dry and ancient. And what did I—no doubt I should say "we"—find in Placide's room, so recently emptied of its clumsy client? Placide, of course. And in the same position in which I had last seen her. Well, the message could not have been more clear, more tender, more demanding, and no sooner did I exchange myself for the missing soldier, thrusting my head into Placide's void—men and women of my nationality are famous for this old-world practice—then up shot Armand, demanding his wicked place between my puckered lips. In the next instant I was all but lost in the motions expected of me, except that it was Armand's head and shoulders and tiny arms—one hand missing—that substituted themselves for my thick tongue. Well, you never heard such a burst of suppressed giggling, such a crescendo of tittering interrupted here and there with rivulets of sweet strangulation that quite put to shame the musical duets of this same modest woman and her husband, the singing master. Placide could not see what was happening to her, could in no way account for such sensations induced, as she thought, by nothing more than one man's own lips and tongue. Astounding! And in no time at all she reached blindly for my head and cried out my name—oh, how I felt Armand squirm at the sound of it, my jealous frog!—and held me, quite breathless, until this uncanny experience faded. Was Armand crushed in the process? For an instant I did not care, but then gradually I became conscious of Armand folding himself back into my mouth and sliding, like nothing so much as a morsel of slimy sea life—an oyster, perhaps—back down into the lair in which he belonged. For hours I felt nothing more from my frog, who must have been curled into a ball and waiting for the recovery that he could not trust to arrive. But even in such a miserable, bruised condition, what grandeur he must have felt, what an escalation of pure amphibious being. Was there another frog in the

world who had so subsumed the man he depended on for
existence? Another frog who had made of himself such a
trickster and who had so intruded into the art of human
love? Never. We give him his due. Yet how he must have
pined for recognition from Placide. How he must have
wished that she had discovered the true source of her
pleasure and expressed her amazement, her gratitude, to
him and not to me. My selfish frog!

Well, the immediate outcome of this encounter was
obvious. Placide became unquenchable. But in addition,
Placide could not keep to herself what had happened.
Thus all the lights began at once to flash, and the days
took their toll. Only with the last of his strength was Armand able to drag himself forth to play his unsuspected
part in the face of expectations that grew ever more demanding. Yet he did so, and not one of those three remaining women failed to be as transported as was Placide.
Amazement was universal in Madame Fromage's establishment, though it was I, of course, on whose shoulders the
honors for this state of things were heaped.

"Pascal?"

"Pascal?"

"Where are you, Pascal?"

But do you know that occasionally, even as Armand
readied himself to assail once again Béatrice or Verveine,
Bluette or Placide, and one of these four rolled onto her
back, even then, when I smelled a perfumed breath and
heard the smiling I could not see, all at once I would
succumb to one of my fits of weeping? Oh yes, cry like a

child, without the slightest reason, my waxen face melting into a mask of idiotic sadness, the sounds of my weeping temporarily blocking Armand's way to his heart's desire and bringing our sport to a standstill. Sometimes, to the utter disappointment of the youngest or oldest, Béatrice or Placide, whoever it was who had summoned me, I gave it all up and, still weeping, in near-blind haste, made my way down the snail's stairwell and out of our hotel and along the empty street to the church.

Of course I have mentioned it already. How could I possibly have forgotten that church? After all, what had I discovered in my religious prowling? Hidden behind that church's altar, except to eyes like mine? A pit of skulls, no less. Exactly!

Let me hasten to add in this same breath, still wet with diminishing tears, that the pit had not been crudely dug, as the word suggests, and was not filled haphazardly with skulls tossed into this odd final resting place with such carelessness that some broke into shards of human pottery while others landed facedown, empty clefts and sockets, once noses and eyes, forever hidden from view. No, this pit had been geometrically prepared, with sheer vertical sides and a pleasing rectangular shape, of a size appropriate only to the number of skulls preserved and then, at last, laid faceup in orderly rows, one atop the other in what I can only call arithmetic tenderness. And among them, there in the uppermost row or lying some- where deep in that mass, whose skull did I see, whether visible or not? My own Maman's, as you have already guessed.

Morbid?

Well, I can only say that though the location of that church was accidental, and accidentally convenient to my needs, still there were times as I crouched peering into that remarkable pit, trying to decide which skull belonged to my dear Maman, when suddenly I wished that between us Armand and I could destroy not only the figments of religion but the syntax—yes, syntax—of human speech. Then we would have no discussions, no arguments, no prayers, no pointing fingers, but instead as many languages as citizens, and all speaking at once, our so-called national discourse reduced to a racket that would make as much sense as my weeping.

And after the solace of such visits, relieved and crouching over and hiding even from myself and Armand, when I inched along the empty streets and returned at last to the foyer in which I had seen that telltale perambulator, what did I find? Exactly. Though perhaps this particular discovery of mine is not so easy to anticipate.

The cap, of course.

In high spirits, then, I would return, unharmed, unmolested, as I would always remind myself. I would stare impatiently at the unlighted switchboard. I would see no lights, hear no footsteps behind me or on the stair. Yet something would cause me to turn about, slowly, as if expecting a blow in the face, and there I would see the cap hanging on a horn of our otherwise empty hatrack and moving, still swaying slightly yet undeniably from where it had been left in its owner's haste. Menacing? Indeed it was. The general whereabouts of its owner would be obvious, but not once—well, yes, once only to be precise—was I tempted to follow him up the spiraling staircase, or to resort to the switchboard to locate his exact threatening presence among our women. You see, I was afraid of him, and just as afraid of his vicious cap. I was simply not man enough to confront the sort of warrior who wears a black cap and parades himself down our avenues in apelike pride. Even a self-tormentor does his best to keep out of harm's way, at least when harm comes to us in such a guise. And Armand? How wrongly I thought of him as being as incapable of heroism as myself.

But as I say, the cap and its missing intruder filled me with a curiosity akin to dread. I wanted nothing to do with either. And so, according to my own scheme of things, confrontation was inevitable. I myself, in all my complexity and weakness, in fact propelled both myself and Armand into the very jaws of arrogance. I admit it freely. Yet how much would I have preferred that no such day had ever arrived and that my frog had continued as the lover he now was and I had been allowed my regimen of cheese, women, and *rognons* prepared especially for me. But where is the vision not meant to be shattered? As in my case it was.

A gray day. A listless day. All women—those, that is, except Placide—occupied in their rooms as usual. Not even Monsieur de La Fayette to draw my ear to the switch-board. Armand dozing, apparently, in a surfeit of plenty. And then? Oh yes, for then suddenly I smelled it, the faintest breath of hair tonic—a man's, of course—and turned and focused on the hatrack my terrible attention. For there it was, the cap! Larger and blacker than ever and still quivering with the haste that had but a moment before left it hanging on the point of one of the great dusty antlers so far from the forest. Once again the cap was there, while its owner, whose head it fit, was already closing the door to room number four and removing his boots, dropping his trousers, smiling at Placide—it could be no other—in all the pretended good nature that was his, while she, poor woman, was already protecting her modesty with that hand of hers to her chest.

Needless to say, Armand was no longer as smug and sluggish as he had been. To the contrary.

As for me, and recognizing this day for what it was—at last and inevitably—slowly I stood up, slowly I abandoned the safety of my post behind the front desk, slowly and in fully acknowledged trepidation I approached that immense black hat, knowing as well as I knew anything what lay in store for me and how much and how swiftly I would regret the moments ahead.

Predictable? Yes, predictable, but nonetheless unavoidable, as we shall see.

Well, in the silence as yet unbroken, and in the shadows as yet undispersed, there I stood within arm's reach of that hat, which, in another instant, and with both hands, I seized. Yes, seized! It was immense, that cap, it rose to a cruel crest in front, its shiny black visor was absurdly small and sharp, nearly vertical, and hence as vicious as a bird's beak. As for its emblem, it was a tarnished silvery thing suggesting some blind bird of prey never to be seen above any natural field and thus all the more fearful.

I summoned the strength and courage to hold in my two hands the invisible intruder's cap. I raised it, as some sweating weight lifter might raise above his head his dumbbells of iron. Then, as Armand set loose a greater than usual burst of pain in my abdomen, I settled that intruder's cap on my head. Yes, purehearted Pascal attempting to don the cap that signaled forth for all to hear its cry of brutality. But can you imagine, large enough for two male heads of ordinary size, as I have said, but too small for me. It was that tight. If the monstrous cap condemned me to its own monstrousness, I, in turn, made the cap, where it perched on my head, ridiculous. Nonetheless I could not tear it swiftly enough from the crown of my head and drop it, fling it down upon the tiles of our foyer, where it landed upside down, where it stayed.

Yet I heard nothing, and Madame Fromage did not open her door so much as a crack to survey this impropriety on her premises.

The rest, I fear, is still more obvious. Having worn his cap, what could I do except follow in the intruder's footsteps? Which is exactly what I did, in an agony of sweat and haste, as Armand trembled in an agitation equal to mine. And paused before the affronting door to Placide's room. Then flung it open, and rushed boldly in upon them, and then abruptly, and reversing my intentions, whatever they might have been, all at once cowered in a corner while Armand, brave Armand, fought for our freedom.

Oh, the impropriety of what I saw! The foreign nakedness. The alien brawn. And Placide as naked as her partner and content, apparently, to be the lesser dog to his larger. Could it be? Bearing his weight and absorbing his sweat and the size of him, literally and euphemistically, that is, concealing whatever pain or anguish she must have felt. Well, such were the surprises that filled my life. Even Armand grew still.

They heard my interruption—how otherwise?— which could not have been more evident than in his scowl and Placide's smile, even in that impossible posture and rude participation that surely would have left the music master speechless.

And I?

Helplessly, violently, quite beside myself, suddenly I vomited into the very eyes of my onlookers! Oh, I might have just been gorging myself on Madame Fromage's cheese, so great was that discharge. And on its crest it carried no other than—of course—Armand!

How then did my enraged frog disport himself? By landing with a terrible determination against that massive buttock closest and uppermost to our view and striking it with a tiny *plop* and, with one hand only, clinging there and hanging on as best he could. Yes, my frog dangling from that sheer buttock like the violent acrobat he was. And how did the great Titan respond? With panic, of course. Not only had he seen a frog vomited from my mouth, as had Placide, and seen it sailing in his direction, but he had felt that tiny unbearable creature sticking to his own bare flesh. Panic indeed, and hardly inseparable from pandemonium, its twin.

In a flash he pulled himself free of Placide and, stumbling over the poor woman too surprised to move, attempted to strike his own buttock, crying out words in a basso voice that neither Placide nor I could understand but we recognized only too well. Whereupon, failing in that first terrified attempt to dislodge the frog that he could not yet force himself to believe in, he now swung himself so violently that Armand—imagine my horror!— lost his hold and, flying off in a dismal arc, fell to the floor. Placide unwittingly called out the name of the music master—Hervé! Hervé!—while her partner, now fully disengaged but still distended, as I could not help but notice, suddenly, to my amazement and increased horror, raised his bare foot and lunged, as if to flatten my frog in one swift ugly blow. But Armand returned immediately to life and, as the monster's foot came down, hopped but a hair to safety. I watched and, as aware of the quizzical look on Placide's face as of the danger that threatened Armand in a contest so apparently unequal, once again saw him rise and soar, not a moment too soon, and with perfect aim strike his enemy exactly where that stunned man was most vulnerable. Again with but one tiny claw he hung dangling as the intruder stood looking down aghast at his own proud male member disfigured by a persistent and impossibly vicious frog. Oh, that disgusting man's dilemma! How rid himself of the frog whose sight and sensation filled him with boyhood revulsion—so much for Henri grown to manhood—if not by a blow of one of his own swarthy hands? But how could he bear to strike that most sensitive part of himself in the process? Was there no other way?

Back came the hand already folded into a fleshy fist, and, decision made and forearm bulging, down he brought the furious blow he could not retrieve. Too late, Titan, for at the last possible minute my daring frog let go, and dropped swiftly and like a stone to the comfort of Placide's mattress, while the human victim stared and drove his intolerable fist directly into his own still-bobbing abomination.

Pain. Frustration. Capitulation. A torrent of that infuriated speech that belonged in our gutters. And even as I cowered, silently cheering Armand for conquering, against all odds, one of our detested intruders, this person, this immense person brought so low at last donned his trousers and guardedly sat out of Armand's way and pulled on his boots. Then, with a scornful look in my direction and with no farewell for Placide, he fled the scene of his humiliation. We listened as the spiraling clatter grew faint. We listened to the slamming door.

Thus we remained, Placide, my frog, and myself. A

larger understanding was beginning to dawn for Placide, by the look on her face. My frog was a hero, though an exhausted one. As for me, I regretted that my days in Madame Fromage's establishment were now over, as in effect they were. Because after all, Madame Fromage would not tolerate the loss of the foreign client I had driven away, scooping up his cap on the run.

But consider the plight of the four women I would leave behind, who, at the outset and thanks to her who had been its witness, could now admit aloud to each other what was all at once impossible yet miraculously true.

Oh, Placide, I cannot live without you!

༞❈༞

CHAPTER FOUR

Lulu

IT WAS NOT LONG before Lulu returned for me. But in the interim of my disgrace, as it was deemed by Madame Fromage, not once did the switchboard beckon me with so much as a glimmer of its orange lights, while even Monsieur de La Fayette failed to answer my soft greeting on those far fewer occasions when he crept past me in the darkness. What helpless anger and even fear must have possessed Madame Fromage, as behind her unmarked door she acknowledged to herself her loss and, as well, wondered whether or not she might yet suffer reprisal. What an unprincipled person she was! And her women? Did they too regret what I had done? After all, and until the very end, that is, it was not for me to know what dear Placide had dared to tell Madame Fromage in explanation of the intruder's flight, or how far she had gone in revealing to her all-eager listeners—Béatrice, Verveine, Bluette—exactly how they, all four of them, had all this while been so delighted by, yes, a frog. Had Placide, in whom I had placed all my trust, withheld the actual source of my frog, describing me as some sort of magician in disguise and thus able to produce my frog on demand, and thereby also treasuring to herself the impossibility of what she had actually seen? Or had she not even comprehended how, indeed, Armand had been able to burst forth into the very episode he had himself destroyed? And no matter what Placide had told the rest or understood herself, except that they all had had relations, so to speak, with a frog, what now were they thinking and feeling in their separate rooms? Revulsion? Defilement? Or only a wan sadness at their present and irreparable state of deprivation, which was like no other?

So we cloaked ourselves in shame that was undeserved, Armand and I, and each in his silence awaited some righting of justice, or the conclusion of the injustice to which we had been condemned. Without cessation I listened to such questions, as maddening to my inner ear as the froglike noise for which there is no cure.

Well, Lulu arrived. Once again I stood as if struck dumb, my crumpled hat on my head, the moment of leave-taking imminent. Madame Fromage did not appear to bid me *adieu* or wish me well, unable as she was to put aside my reprehensible behavior, as she considered it, or to face me in the light of her unadmitted responsibility for allowing that man or those men who were not our countrymen into the rooms of her girls. And then? Yes, then, just as Lulu was opening the door to the street, all at once there came a rustling from the stairway, and in the next moment, there I stood surrounded by Placide, Béatrice, Bluette, Verveine, holding closed the negligees that but partially concealed the undergarments of their professions. They smiled, they allowed themselves no more than a few whispered words. But they were enough.

"*Merci,* Pascal!"

"*Merci!* . . ."

"*Merci!* . . ."

Even I am unable to admit to the despondency I felt on that familiar train, as if both that train and I knew full well that never again would I be one of its passengers or travel except on foot beyond Saint-Mamès to its nearby village. Needless to say, Maman's rose-strewn casket was no longer locked in the compartment adjoining ours.

So I sat facing Lulu, my eyes down, my hat in my hands. Why could I not have been proud of myself? Why could I not have summoned my usual pride in Armand, especially since he, insignificant creature, had routed the enemy? But of Lulu there was no doubt. I had failed him, I did not deserve his patience or his usual protection. And yet, I began to realize, Lulu did not share my somber view of myself. In fact, swaying heavily across from me during that long ride back to where I belonged, Lulu, though he did not speak, was smiling, or all but smiling, as if he knew in secret that there was more awaiting me at Saint-Mamès than the malice of Dr. Chapôte. Lulu's secret— for that's what it was—became swiftly enough my own.

Lulu guided me at once and as a matter of course to the director himself, where he sat, as had become his habit in my absence, at the empty table in the very dining room that once, thanks to my culinary art, had been the scene

of his feasting as well as the only period in his married
life when he had found himself loving his wife and enjoying his role as husband. Now Dr. Chapôte did not raise
his eyes to me and was, as I saw at once, a man even more
despondent than myself.

Marie-Claude was gone and would never return,
which he knew and I knew, doctor and patient swathed
alike in her absence.

So I took for myself the bedchamber that had once
been Marie-Claude's, and took for myself Dr. Chapôte's
personal study, little enough compensation for what I had
lost and the exclusion I had been made to feel at last from
all the dim shapes and shadows reachable only outside
Saint-Mamès, where I was, and am, to spend my life—
because of a happy childhood and an aging frog who now
had become so dormant that I longed to feel again the
pain that he could cause me.

Finally, and for no reason, Lulu decided that it was
time to take mercy on Pascal and his frog. One early evening he discovered me still downcast and doing nothing
in the doctor's study, and beckoned me to follow him into
the soft light that awaited us. There was no breeze, it was
pleasantly cool, Saint-Mamès might have been empty, so
placid was the calm that had settled on its fields that
stretched as far as the distant filigree of trees which in turn
proceeded on into a wood we could not see and which
came to no end. Somehow the light had achieved a balance that would not change, for the moment at least.

We turned down a sanded alleyway. Lulu unlocked a

wooden door. We entered a stone enclosure with high walls and no roof, and remote—how peacefully remote! —from that very Saint-Mamès in which it was hidden. Empty, as I first thought? Oh, anything but empty, as Lulu and I stood together and surveyed the scene before us, and Armand stirred.

A dozen or more inmates like myself, yet vastly more fortunate, all moving in a placid circle, and stooping at the waist, and following, the lot of them—what else?— their frogs! Yes, each person was accompanied by his or her own frog, and not only were these frogs, large and small, golden or reddish, moving as if to take much-needed exercise, but, now and again, were hopping over each other! Soaring and being soared over!

Of course there was no keeping Armand in the darkness that was myself. Up he must come, and did, and even while Lulu leaned against the wall and watched us, my frog leapt into that procession of frogs, while I, bending forward like the others, joined the proud owners of these for the moment liberated creatures hopping, leaping, filling the still air with their croaking.

Evening after evening I joined the men and women who assembled, or were assembled one by one by Lulu, and then as delicately as possible turned away their heads and raised and cupped their hands and into them dis-charged their own distinctive frogs. Never did we mistake someone else's frog for our own; by some shared instinct we followed along in silent harmony, except for the crude singing of the frogs, and took each of our steps carefully enough, I can tell you. I was not curious. I asked Lulu for no explanation. It was evident that in my absence he had made his astounding discovery, which was that among all those sequestered in Saint-Mamès, there were others like myself, and frogs like Armand.

Thanks to Lulu we now recognize each other. Thanks to him we congregate inside his secret. And each and every evening our frogs are joined by other frogs, though there is not a frog pond in sight.

Thus I am not so very different, after all, from my countrymen. I am not alone. What more do I need to begin my tale?

Maman! Maman! I can live without you!

CHAPTER FIVE

※

Pascal Gâteau

LITTLE IS KNOWN about this person except his name and that he died in one of our oldest asylums in a mysterious choking fit when he was not yet forty years old. At the instant of death his hands flew to his throat, he fell to earth, writhed a moment or two, and was gone. Much later, probing fingers intending to dislodge whatever might have been stuck in his throat found nothing.

It is the kind of event that most invites our speculation.

Something other than inexplicable contractions of the throat caused this person's death. Very well. Let us make the wildest possible assumptions. Let us suppose that Pascal Gâteau choked to death not on a bone or a morsel of free-floating food or on one of his own teeth come loose, but on an obstruction which itself drew breath.

An obstruction that breathed? That was as alive as the very person it destroyed? Oh, but we are indulging in the logic of purely wayward fantasies, as I say.

First a few eliminations. Monsieur Gâteau did not strangle to death on a bird, no matter how small. Nor on any form of, say, lizard, since that species of creature is not known for its bulk. A bat is a possibility, yet is too birdlike and, even for us thinkers, far-fetched. Well, then, why not a frog? After all, it is only a justifiable invention. An exercise in reason, if you will.

So let us imagine that somehow a frog, a particular frog, managed to enjoy a relationship of sorts with said Pascal Gâteau throughout that person's life, short as it was. Let us assume that in general, harmony existed between the two. But let us also assume that "marriages" of this or any kind are never invulnerable to disruption with or without cause. Very well. If our frog had gained access to the mouth or throat of Monsieur Gâteau—please! we need not explain everything!—and one day simply found itself possessed of a sudden spite after the passing of so many years, but also with a sudden burst of inspiration, might it not have thrust itself into an appropriate place in the throat and swelled? There we have it. The surprise. The helplessness. The terrible strangulation of Pascal Gâteau.

Ah, but let us think of the frog. Think of the frog's pain, I beg you, which must result from the man's explosive choking and the involuntary constricting of the throat in a blind effort to dislodge the obstruction. Slowly this Monsieur Gâteau's breath would be closed off, like water in a tap, but at the same time the obstructor, this frog, would suffer an all but intolerable crushing.

So we have the hands flying to the throat, the eyes bursting, as it were, and the body crashing to earth, and so forth. The point is that the frog did not stay where it was, or it would have been found. So what then became of Monsieur Gâteau's frog?

We may say that the creature, with no regrets for its crime—the illogical revenge it had enacted on poor Gâteau—even at death's door managed to pull itself from the windpipe reduced to but half its size. What a painful endeavor. Yet thus exactly did the mortally injured frog escape and slip away and, like one of our famous supplin-ants, drag on until at last it found a crevice or hole in the earth into which it could creep and there, flattened and disfigured and undiscovered, die.

How else explain the unnatural death of Monsieur Pascal Gâteau? Or, who is to say that what is here described did not happen? Never, never underestimate the power of clear thinking!

"Well, my dear," said the old lady, closing the book and addressing the man who had the day long awaited this moment in attentive silence, "I withdraw my reservations. It is a charming tale. But I will tell you one thing. I shall forbid my great-grandchildren the slightest proximity to frogs!"